THE SEASONS OF A HEART

The Seasons of a Heart

Constance O. Irvin

iUniverse, Inc.
New York Lincoln Shanghai

The Seasons of a Heart

iUniverse books may be ordered through booksellers or by contacting:

iUniverse
2021 Pine Lake Road, Suite 100
Lincoln, NE 68512
www.iuniverse.com
1-800-Authors (1-800-288-4677)

ISBN-13: 978-0-595-35475-7 (pbk)

ISBN-13: 978-0-595-79967-1 (ebk)

ISBN-10: 0-595-35475-0 (pbk)

ISBN-10: 0-595-79967-1 (ebk)

Printed in the United States of America

Dedication:

To my father who gave me wings,
To my mother who grounded me,
To my brother who taught me to compete,
And to my sister who simply loves me.

CHAPTER 1

In the dead of winter, there is no colder place than Chicago with its winds that sweep across Lake Michigan, bringing bone-chilling temperatures and wildly swirling snow. For that reason, Diana Forrester dreaded getting out of the taxi as it stopped in front of the terminal at Midway Airport. She pulled her wool scarf around her neck while the driver waited for his fare.

He held out his hand. "Helluva evening for flying."

She nodded. "Yeh, maybe I'll be lucky and it won't go."

He looked at the money and then at her. "Thanks. You have a safe journey. Smile for your passengers."

Diana stepped out into ankle deep snow on the sidewalk. As she dragged her flight bag behind her, the wheels skidded recklessly in the slush. "Damn," she muttered to herself. She struggled with the terminal door, jerked the flight bag inside and headed toward the crew's lounge for Drake Airlines. When she approached the check-in desk, Mary looked up and smiled at her.

"Evening, Diana. Some weather, huh?"

Diana stopped at the counter. "Yeh, it's Chicago. Are there many passengers?"

"About a dozen or so."

"Is the flight leaving on time?"

Mary rolled her eyes. "I'm not real sure of that. Mr. Drake and Frank are in the hangar discussing something about the plane."

Diana arched an eyebrow. "Discussing something about the plane? Like what?"

"I'm not sure. Frank said maybe there was a problem, but he didn't say what."

"Oh, God. Just let me get through until spring with this airline and then I'm headed for parts unknown and I'll be unfound."

Mary laughed. "That sounds exciting."

"I hope so and I hope it's warm, with sunny beaches. See you later."

Mary called after her. "You bet. I'm doing the security check for the flight too."

Diana shook her head as she entered the crew lounge. Drake would use people in six different positions, if he could get away with it. "Cheap," she thought. "Except for things he wants, like eight dollar cigars."

Sam Nichols, the pilot was seated at a table, drinking some coffee with his co-pilot, Randy Mattson. They both looked up as she entered.

"Hey, girl. Glad you're with us tonight."

Her grey blue eyes twinkled at the sight of Sam. "Thanks." She sat down at the table with the two men. On the wall behind Randy's head, a Miss January pin-up girl smiled back at her from an Acme Disposal calendar. She hated those stupid poses and the affront of the pictures, but Carl Drake loved "to look at them", so there they stayed. It wasn't that she didn't like women, she did, but somehow they cheapened how she felt about herself and the women she had loved.

"Why do I always face those things? Isn't anyone else bothered by them?"

"Yeh, they bother me something terrible, that's why I don't face 'em. It's hard to concentrate on the upcoming flight if I get them on my mind." Sam winked at Randy.

"Okay, wise guys. So what's the deal with the plane?"

Sam tensed a little. "I don't know. I heard a loud argument between Frank and Carl. Frank was real mad. I couldn't make out what was said though. Carl popped his head in the door a minute ago and said the flight would be half an hour late."

"Oh. Any reason given?"

"Hell, no. You know Carl. He wouldn't let on anything was wrong with any of his birds. God must be with us. Those planes are accidents waiting to happen. Frank works like a dog to keep them safe, but you know Carl. Stretch the rules. One day the FAA will have a field day with Drake Airlines." Sam finished his coffee and rolled the Styrofoam cup along the edge of the yellowing Formica tabletop.

Randy stared at the door to the hangar. "Kind of scary for me. You two have been with this airline for years. I'm not used to it yet."

Sam smiled. "Ah, don't mind us. We just have burnout. Most aren't like this. You'll graduate, Randy. Diana and I just want a few more years and then, poof...gone."

"I only want a few more months and I'm gone. No more flying for me. At least not as a stewardess." Diana got up from the table and opened the door into the passenger area. She took a quick look and then turned back toward Sam and Randy just as the door from the hangar area opened with a bang.

Carl Drake, a short, rotund man, entered the room, his dark eyes almost hidden in a face puffed up with anger. He reached inside his suit coat pocket and extracted a *Macanudo* cigar. He relaxed.

"Well, Sam, it looks like you'll have to fly after all. The bird is ready to go. No problem. Frank fixed it up just fine. He had a long day, so I let him go home." Carl smiled at Diana and then took a pocketknife from his pants pocket. He carefully cut the end of the cigar, then ran it under his nose to smell the aroma. It made him smile.

Sam brightened. "Great. What about Madison? Any passengers?"

"No. That should help you make up some time. Just a straight shot to Duluth." Carl paused to light his cigar. "I checked with flight service about ten minutes ago. They're predicting light snow and moderate northeasterly winds. Piece of cake." He blew a large smoke ring. The circle drifted lazily upward.

Sam finished his cigarette and stood up. "Yeh, I checked too. Sounds like nothing but clear sailing." He moved toward the door. "Come on, Randy. Help me drag the ole girl out."

Randy got up from the table and approached the door.

Sam turned back to Diana and said, "It'll take us about ten minutes. No use in you getting out in the cold before you have to."

"Thanks, Sam. You're always gallant." She smiled at the two men. Diana was especially fond of Sam.

Sam winked at her and he and Randy went into the hangar area. Diana and Carl were left alone in the room. Diana was never comfortable around Carl, particularly if she was alone with him, as now. She looked aimlessly at the wall and was miffed by the calendar girls.

Carl had poured himself a cup of coffee. He slurped at it. "How's my favorite girl?"

"If you mean me, I'm fine."

"You bet you are, kid." He slurped another mouthful. "You aren't still planning to leave us, are you?"

Diana took relish in her answer. "In the spring, yes." She got up from the table and moved away from Carl toward the coat rack and got her coat.

"I just can't figure out what a good looking woman like you finds so damn interesting in a bunch of bugs and weeds."

"You forget. I grew up with bugs and weeds. I like them even better than some people I know." She walked toward the door to the passenger area and continued, "I'd better get the passengers prepared to board. Good evening, Mr. Drake."

"Yeh, sure. Good evening."

Diana entered the waiting room of Drake Airlines. The room reflected years of quick paint jobs, sloppy with lack of detail. The chairs for the passengers had been taken from some theatre that had long since been shut down. They were make-do, nothing comfortable about them. Vending machines lined the right wall, their fronts dirty with fingerprints and spilled drinks. Diana mentally counted fifteen passengers, including a small child, who was sleeping in a scrunched position on one of the hard wooden seats. A dark-complected man banged on the coffee machine to retrieve his money, making it necessary for Diana to shout.

"I need everyone's attention, please."

The Chicano stopped banging and the others spent a few moments gathering their belongings around them. They looked intently at Diana.

"We will be boarding for our flight to Duluth shortly. The pilot and co-pilot are giving the plane a final check now. Please take care of any last minute phone calls or any other arrangements you might need to make."

The passengers came to life and began moving about the waiting room with anticipation. The Chicano approached Diana. "Hey, what was the holdup, anyway? I don't like this. See? I got a funeral to go to."

"It was nothing really. Just a minor problem. We won't be stopping in Madison. That will put the flight to Duluth just about on schedule." She smiled at the man.

He flashed a broad smile back. "Say, you're okay."

The outside door crashed open and Randy entered the passenger area. Behind him, the sound of an engine whined loud in the cold air. Falling snow followed him into the room. He approached Diana.

"We're all set, Di. Just remind them that the one fired up engine on the right side will be kicking up a little snow. Get them aboard as quickly as possible. I'll go get security to check them through X-ray and metal detection."

The passengers began jockeying for position closest to the machines that would allow them access to the plane.

"Okay people, this is it. Once you're through security, go directly to the plane where the co-pilot will help you aboard. There's plenty of room. One engine is running, and it's kicking up some snow. Watch your step. Be careful." Diana began checking flight tickets.

Randy returned with Mary from the front counter in tow.

"Here I am again. Double duty." Mary smiled as she took her position next to the walk through metal detector.

One by one the passengers walked through the detector and continued out to the waiting plane. The Chicano stepped through the metal loop and the machine buzzed loudly.

"Hey, what the hell is that?" He looked perplexed.

Mary stopped him and said politely. "Step back, please, and empty your pockets."

"What the hell for?"

"It's the law. You must have something metal in your pockets. And more than just change. Empty them on the counter or don't get on the plane."

Diana moved closer to the small counter next to the detector.

The Chicano looked sheepish. "Don't get excited. I ain't never flown before. What's the big deal?" He emptied the contents of his pants pockets on the counter. A large switchblade stuck out like a proverbial sore thumb among all the change.

Mary's eyes widened. Diana picked it up and looked at it. "You can't carry this thing aboard the airplane. Let me see your ticket."

He handed her his ticket and she looked at his name.

The Chicano laughed. "Hey, I don't go nowhere without it. You ever been on Clark Street, lady? The north side of Chicago? Hell, a looker like you'd need six of those to fight off Hispanics like me." He laughed again.

"Maybe I would, Mr. Urbano Rivera, but this isn't Clark Street. And, I can't let you carry it aboard the plane." She smiled politely.

"Hey, look. I ain't no hijacker. I'll tell you what. You keep it for me. Okay? Just give it to me when we get there. I gotta have it. It's like a friend. I been carrying it since I was ten. See what I mean?"

She studied his face. "Yeh, I see. You'll get it back. I promise." She returned his ticket to him.

During this exchange, the other passengers had proceeded through the security check until only few remained. A woman in her mid thirties moved up behind Urbano as he walked through the checkpoint.

Urbano winked at Diana. "You're okay, lady." He turned slightly back toward the woman behind him and said, "Chicks, they all go for the soft side." He chuckled to himself as he bent his head into the wind and swaggered his way to the plane.

The woman handed her ticket to Diana and gave her briefcase to Mary for X-Ray. "This should be an interesting trip."

Diana handed back the ticket and looked directly into the most unusual eyes she had ever seen. The woman's eyes were almost violet in color. Her perfume stirred a momentary feeling within Diana. She felt her face slightly flush and tried to mask the reaction. "Oh, yeh. Him. Harmless. I think."

The woman retrieved her briefcase and made her way to the waiting twin engine plane. Diana stared after her and wondered about the blond woman with the violet eyes. It seemed that those eyes had looked right through her. Maybe it was the color that had so startled her. Or maybe the perfume. Maybe both.

Mary spoke. "Well, that's it."

"Oh, yes." Diana looked around the empty waiting room. "Catch you on the return flight tomorrow. Have a good one for me, Mary. Bye."

"See ya. Have a good flight."

Diana scurried toward the Mohawk 298. The lone engine whined loud. She quickly mounted the steps, and with the help of Randy, slammed the door shut. The warmth of the small cabin area felt good. The other engine coughed and sputtered and then kicked into the same high pitched whine as the first. Diana knew that shortly, they would be airborne toward Duluth. She made her way back through the aisle and prepared the passengers for take-off. The blond woman was seated next to Urbano near the tail section of the plane. Diana smiled at the contrast of personalities seated next to one another.

CHAPTER 2

Inside the cockpit area, Sam and Randy ran down a pre-flight checklist. Randy threw switches as Sam read from the list and then he turned them off again. Each time he answered, "Check." Sometimes the warning lights would let them know of a malfunction and they would have to hold the flight for further checks by one of their two mechanics. Tonight they both hoped they would get through the list without a hitch.

Finally, Sam said, "Okay, Randy. That's it. Everything checks out. Just another day in paradise." Randy eased back in his seat. Sam turned to look toward Diana, who waited inside the small cockpit area.

"Is the door secure? Passengers belted?"

"You bet, Sam. All set to go?"

"Yeh, all the right lights came on. No hitches."

Diana liked the easiness of Sam. He made flights feel safe, even when she knew that Carl Drake bent the rules on safety for his airplanes. She turned toward the passenger area a few steps and stood near a small seat just inside the cockpit area. She reached for a mike and took it from its bracket on the cabin wall.

"Please check your seatbelts and remember there is no smoking during our flight. Weather permitting; I will serve coffee, drinks and light snacks once we reach cruise altitude. Our flight this evening will take us about three hours. Thank you." She returned the mic to its bracket and sat down on the jump seat and belted herself in.

Sam had already begun to rev up the engines. He spoke into his headset. "Midway ground control…Drake niner-three is ready to taxi. Instruments to Duluth. Over."

A voice came back over the radio. "Flight niner-three, say again. There was a break in your transmission. Over."

Sam frowned as he repeated. "Midway Ground control, this is niner-three, ready to taxi. IFR to Duluth. Over."

"Reading you loud and clear flight niner-three. Runway three one left. Wind zero three zero at fifteen, gusting to zero two five. Light snow……"

Sam started the run to the designated runway, while Randy continued to monitor the instruments. The engines sounded smooth. Light snow pelted the windshield. Outside, the ground crews were busy keeping the runways clear and devoid of ice. Flight niner-three turned off the taxiway and on to runway three-one left. Sam pushed the dual throttles full ahead and the plane roared down the runway and lifted air ward.

In spite of the snow, Chicago at night was ablaze with millions of different twinkling colored lights. Sam loved to see Chicago like that. It reminded him of a miniature railroad town he had built for his O gauge railroad when he was a teenager. He absolutely delighted in the sight of it.

Randy flipped off the running lights as the plane reached near cruising altitude. Sam smiled. "Almost time for coffee."

"You bet. And some pretzels." Randy laughed.

Inside the cabin, Diana had already unbuckled her lap belt. She made her way to the rear of the plane where a small galley area contained a coffee urn and a refrigerator full of assorted pop and juice. An upper cabinet held tiny bottles of liquor and an array of various small bags of pretzels and candy bars. She carried a basket of pretzels down the aisle and distributed them to the passengers. Most of the passengers wanted coffee, which she got out quickly, with the help of Randy, who had come up from the cockpit to assist her. When the chore was almost done, he returned to the cockpit with two cups of steaming coffee.

Diana now began the task of handing out pop and liquor to the few who wanted it. Urbano had wanted a coke and some rum. He and the woman with violet eyes were seated on the right, at the rear of the plane near the galley. The woman, who had the aisle seat, was busy reading some sort of report. She did not even look up as Diana brushed against her while handing Urbano his drink. Diana moved down the aisle to serve another passenger.

As she moved away, Urbano said without thinking, "Nice ass."

The woman looked up. "What?"

"The chick. Nice ass. Yeh?"

"I really didn't notice." She went back to her reading.

Urbano sensed her annoyance. "Hey, lady. I didn't mean no harm, really. Just dumb talk, you know?"

She smiled at him. "Yes, I know." She turned back to the report.

Urbano looked at her a moment. "You fly a lot, lady?"

"Yes. Business trips mostly."

"I thought so. You don't seem nervous. Me, I ain't never been flyin' before. Wouldn't now, except for a funeral. Hell of a time to die. Dead of winter." He drank slowly from his rum and coke.

She was not sure what to say to this stranger, so she said nothing. She returned to her reading, while Urbano continued to sip from his drink.

When Diana finished serving drinks, she returned to the small aft galley to clean up the area and to make a note of items that would need replenished. She checked her watch and noted that they had been aloft for over an hour and a half. She glanced forward. Some of the passengers slept. A small child, a girl, was singing a Christmas song. Her mother tried to hush her, but the child only softened the volume, and continued to sing.

The engines droned on. There was a slight change in their sound and Diana looked forward. She was not sure what she heard, but it seemed different. She made a mental note to asked Sam about the change, but for now, she concentrated on the inventory in the galley and dismissed what her ears had heard.

In the cockpit, Sam and Randy were busy checking instruments. Randy tapped on the glass of the tachometer.

"Damn. There is a drop in RPMs, Sam."

"I know. I felt and heard it. Check the wings and see if ice is forming. We've lost a couple hundred feet in altitude along with the drop in RPMs." Sam studied the instruments, while Randy retrieved a flashlight from his flight briefcase.

Randy unbuckled his harness and turned to the right and flashed the beam upward toward the overhead right wing. The plane suddenly buffeted downward. Randy grabbed the arm of his seat and steadied himself. "I can't see anything out there. It's snowing too hard." He quickly reharnessed his safety belt.

Sam struggled with the yoke and felt a momentary sense of relief as the plane steadied itself. "The RPM's are still dropping. Hit the carb heat, Randy."

Randy did as instructed. Both he and Sam studied the dual instruments. There was no increase in RPM's.

"Dammit, Randy. Activate the de-icer boots. We don't have carburetor icing. There must be ice forming on the wings."

Randy flipped the carb heat switch to off and turned the de-icer switch to on. He strained to see outside. "Shit. I can't tell if they worked. I don't think the boots inflated." He turned back to Sam just as the lights flickered in the cockpit. Out of the corner of his eye, he saw the altimeter drop another 300 feet.

Sam struggled with the yoke. "Turn the switch off. Wait ten seconds and try again."

Randy performed the task and waited. He turned the de-icer on again, but nothing happened. The plane continued to drop altitude. "They're not inflating, Sam. Something is really wrong."

Sam ignored FAA rules about swearing. He knew the cockpit recorder taped everything, but he was afraid and he no longer cared to be polite. "Those son of a bitchin' weather reports. Light snow, huh? What's our ETA for Duluth?"

Randy pulled his airman's calculator from his briefcase and made a few rotations. "About another hour. Of course, we may have had an increase in wind velocity. Want me to check with in-flight service?"

Sam pushed forward on the throttles to increase power. "Yeh, call ahead to Duluth and see what the weather is like there. We must have had an unexpected change."

Randy punched in the frequency for in-flight service and pulled the mike on his headset closer. "Duluth flight service. This is Drake Niner three requesting Duluth weather. Over."

He waited. The radio response was garbled. Only a few words were audible. "Flight......transmission......cannot......say...Duluth......"

"Could you make any of that out, Sam?" Randy began to perspire.

"No. Try again."

Randy's voice pleaded into the mike. "Duluth flight service. This is Drake Niner three requesting Duluth weather. Over."

The plane dropped altitude and Sam struggled even more with the yoke.

In the cabin area, a coffee cup toppled off an old woman's tray. She squeaked in alarm. The man beside her jumped awake with a start. "Stewardess. What the hell is going on?"

Diana had tried for several minutes to steady herself in the galley area. She knew that something was definitely wrong with the flight. She had already started forward when the man's words stopped her. She smiled down at him. "No problem, sir. Just a little rough weather. Nothing to worry about." She stooped and retrieved the cup from the aisle. She moved forward to the cockpit and closed the door between the passengers and the cockpit.

Sam turned slightly toward her. "Hi, Di."

"What's going on, Sam?"

"We've got ice on the wings and a slight radio problem. But, I think we can handle it. Make sure the passengers tighten their seat belts and you'd better secure yourself."

Diana frowned. "That bad?" She looked from Sam to Randy. Randy looked away.

Sam continued. "The weather has deteriorated, but we can't go back. We're closing in on Duluth. Besides, I've never had to turn tail yet and I'm not about to. We'll make it." He paused. "Prepare them for some bumpy spots."

Diana opened the door. "Okay, Sam. I'll take care of them. Just get us home free."

Sam gave her a thumbs up signal and she turned to face the passengers. She saw the fear in their faces as she closed the door. Even the woman with the violet eyes stared at her with a pleading look. Urbano had covered his face with his hands. Diana saw a rosary dangling between his fingers. She moved slowly toward the rear of the plane, quietly giving instructions as she went.

CHAPTER 3

"Why didn't you tell her that we lost radio contact and that the nav system is screwy?"

Sam did not answer Randy. He hit a switch and a grinding mechanical sound echoed through the cockpit.

"Sam, I am not even sure where we are." Randy fumbled with a calculator and a nav chart. Fear gripped his face.

"Get a hold of yourself. I've dropped the flaps to try to break ice away."

Randy wiped sweat off his forehead. "Will that solve our problem?"

"Not really. We can't make Duluth." Sam turned and looked at the chart Randy held. "What about Gogebic County airport. Are we close at all?"

Randy moved his finger along the chart and glanced at his watch and then the airspeed indicator. "Gogebic is too far away. I think we're closer to Hayward. They have a five thousand foot runway and they've got Unicom. Only it's not manned at night."

Sam struggled with the yoke and the plane lurched violently. Screams came from the cabin area.

"Hayward's an omni station, isn't it?"

Randy nodded a `yes'.

Sam continued. "See if you can get their signal. I don't know where we are at all. The nav system is totally shot."

Randy switched a navigational dial and turned to Sam. "I'm on the frequency. Do you show anything?"

"No, and there's no audible station I.D. We're in a lot of trouble buddy." Sam bit his lip. "Get out a Mayday. I can't hold her. We're going down."

For a moment Randy looked at Sam in disbelief. The cabin lights flickered and snapped Randy back to movement. He nervously turned the radio to 121.5, the emergency frequency, and adjusted his headset.

"Mayday. Mayday. Flight Niner three. Mayday."

A smell of burning electrical wires seeped into the cockpit. Blinding snow buffeted the plane. Sam flipped on the landing lights and for a second, the lights stabbed at the swirling snow, but then they abruptly went out. Sam pushed the throttles forward, but there was no response from the engines.

Randy continued. "Mayday. Mayday. Flight Niner three. Mayday." There was a pleading, begging sound to the words.

The lights in the cockpit flickered and went out. The right engine sputtered. Whined. Revved up. Sputtered and stopped. The power of the still running left engine pulled the plane to the left. Sam frantically made adjustments, but the yoke was sloppy and without much response. Sam knew there was no use to fight it anymore. He relaxed his grip. He instinctively looked toward the altimeter, but could not see what the gauge registered because total darkness enveloped the aircraft. Next to him, Randy still pleaded into the mike. Sam reached over and feathered the left engine. Silence encased the airplane.

In the darkness, Randy spoke. "Why'd you do that?"

"Because, Randy. I have done all I could. I can't stop what is happening to us. I have to try to ease it down, so maybe some people will survive."

Randy could not see Sam's face, but something about the calm, precise way that he spoke made Randy pull off his headset. He put his hands on the yoke in front of him. "I'll help, Sam. Nobody is listening, anyway."

There was an eerie, almost mystical silence as the craft sank earthward. Then, muffled praying came from the cabin area. The small child cried. Neither Sam, nor Randy spoke to one another again. When the plane banked slightly to the left, the top of a fir tree came into Sam's view. He gripped the yoke as tight as he could. As the plane dropped lower and crashed through the forest, the praying became screams, and pleading for God to have mercy.

Tree branches shattered the cockpit windows and stabbed at both Sam and Randy. The left wing was sheared off by the heavy trunks of oak, maple and white pine. The plane continued to cut a path through the dense woods. Part of the right wing snapped off as it hit a large boulder and the fuselage proceeded to plow a furrow into the heavily drifted snow. Tree branches pealed the left rear section of the plane's body off its frame. Finally, the forward motion was halted by an irrevocable smashing into rocks and trees. The grinding, deafening noise of the dying plane was all but obliterated by the howling wind.

Then, there was only the sound of the wind.

Snow swirled through the gaping hole in the left side of the aircraft. The wind pushed it inside toward the galley area in the rear of the cabin where a piece of shredded clothing clung to part of the mangled airframe and flapped noisily like a ripped sail in a gale. A low moan sounded above the howling of the wind.

"Jesus, Mary, Mother of God," Urbano said. He rubbed his head and felt the warmth of blood. He poked at the woman. "Hey, lady. You okay?"

The woman with the violet eyes roused. "Oh, my God. Yes. Yes. I'm okay. We should get out of here."

"Yeh, lady, sure." Urbano unbuckled his safety belt and tried to stand. His legs buckled and he sank down to the seat again.

The woman stood up just as a moan sounded somewhere behind their seat. She moved over debris toward the sound and knelt down. "Let me help you."

Diana struggled to get free of her jump seat. The harness buckle was twisted. Her hands were slightly cut and the cold had made her fingers all but useless. The woman pulled and tugged at the buckle and it finally gave way.

Diana stood on rubbery legs. "I'm all right. We'd better see to the others." She groped her way in the darkness to the galley and rummaged in a cabinet for the emergency flashlight.

The woman spoke. "My name is Casey Morgan. What's yours?"

"Diana. Diana Forrester." She located the flashlight and switched it on. The beam illuminated Casey's face and Diana saw a large knot on her forehead. "Are you okay?"

"Yes, but the man next to me is cut."

"Urbano?"

"Yes, I guess that's his name." She turned back to him and in doing so, now, under the light, saw the carnage forward in the plane. "Oh, my." She gasped in fright as she covered her face with her hands and turned her back to the scene. She stumbled toward the gaping hole, retching as she went.

Diana moved to Urbano first and looked at his head. He moaned. "Let me look closer." She sat down on the seat next to him and pulled his bloody hands from his head. The cut was only superficial, but as with most head wounds, the blood had flowed freely. The cold air had already stopped the flow.

"How bad is it, lady?"

"Don't worry. It's a small cut. Nothing really. You'll be all right."

Urbano stood up and looked forward. "Jesus. Let me out of here." He pushed past her and Casey and made his way to the rear exit. He jumped out into the snow.

Diana had been trained to deal with accidents, but the devastation of the wreck momentarily overwhelmed her. She took several deep breaths to stop her head and stomach from reacting to what her eyes saw. She whispered to herself as she moved forward toward an old man. "Oh, God, his face is gone." She moved from side to side, taking time to try to get a pulse from any who appeared as though they might have life. None did.

Casey remained with her back to the carnage.

Outside, Urbano paced nervously a few steps in one direction and then reversed his steps. Back and forth. Back and forth. Finally he yelled. "Hey, where the hell are we?" He blew warm air on his freezing hands. "Goddamit, where are we?"

No one answered him. Diana stood in the entrance to the cockpit. Bits and pieces of tree limbs were jammed into the sidewalls. A large limb had pierced Sam's neck. His eyes stared, unseeing. His hands tightly gripped the yoke. Randy had suffered a spear like wound through the heart. He too stared, but saw nothing.

Tears welled in Diana's eyes. She had known Sam for almost five years. He had become her favorite pilot and Randy, the boy like man, had made her smile with his silly jokes and ready laughter. She wiped the tears from her eyes. There was no time for sorrow, for her task was to tend to the living.

"Hey, where the hell are we?" Urbano sounded frantic.

Diana moved back down the cluttered aisle, averting her eyes from the bodies that surrounded her and yelled to him. "I don't know, but they'll find us. We'll wait here." She had reached Casey now, and the woman turned toward her.

Casey spoke, "We should get away from the plane. It might catch on fire."

"No, not now. It won't now. We have to stay with the plane. That's our only hope. Help me get some things to protect us from the cold. Check the overhead bins for blankets. Coats. Anything that looks warm." Diana moved to the exit doorway and shined the light outside on Urbano.

Urbano was pacing, his bare hands tucked under his armpits. "Jesus, it's dark. No lights. No houses. Nothing."

"Come in Urbano and help us. Everyone else is gone. We have to get together whatever we can to protect ourselves until rescuers come."

He looked up at Diana with a mixture of fear and anger. "I'm not coming in there with dead guys. Stiffs make me nervous." He blew his warm breath on his cold hands.

"You'll be stiff yourself, if you don't get out of the wind. Now help us."

Urbano moved toward the gaping hole and peered in. The flashlight seemed to wander at will as Diana checked bins and helped Casey pile blankets and coats on seats near the galley. A gust of wind blew a coating of thin snow on Urbano's face. His nose instantly dripped with mucus. He wiped it with his cold hand. The blankets looked less frightening than the thought of death, and so, he struggled on the cold metal of the plane to pull himself inside. Diana heard him and came to offer her hand. His eyes showed his fear, but he let her pull him up into the shattered remains of Flight Niner three.

Diana, Casey and Urbano huddled together in a seat that had been ripped from its anchorage and tossed slightly aft of the galley. That section of the fuselage had remained intact and offered a protection from the wind. There was no thought that they would not huddle this closely together. Each knew that their life depended on warmth and that warmth would come from another. There was no thought that help would not come. Each believed that help would come tomorrow. In the cold and in the shadow of death, exhausted and emotionally drained, they finally fell asleep.

Outside the wind howled and the snow continued to fall. Somewhere in the distance there was a howl that was not the wind. It bore the sound of some primal animal seeking a lost mate. The howl blended in with the wilderness and became a part of the night and a sad mourning sound that could not awaken all who might hear it. The cry came again and was answered by another. Then, there was only the howl of the wind. And the night passed.

CHAPTER 4

The snowfall during the night had been heavy and so, by the dawning of the following morning, the aircraft was virtually obscured by snow. It was so covered by drifts and fallen pine and spruce branches that even someone on foot, within fifty yards of it, would have a hard time seeing that it was a downed plane. The wind had subsided during the night, but now the falling snow increased in volume. The large heavy flakes drifted lazily and settled on everything. Near the plane, the debris from the crash had formed small humps and bumps underneath the drifts. Some of the humps were suitcases and some were pieces of twisted metal, or seat cushions, and some were human bodies. The snow covered it all, making it clean.

Urbano stirred underneath the mound of makeshift covers of airline blankets and an assortment of coats. He moved out from the warmth and stumbled over clutter to the hole in the side of the plane and looked outside.

"I thought you said they'd find us. Shit. They won't find nothin' in this place. We're gonna die." He lit a cigarette. "Then we'll look like them." He pointed to the dead bodies inside the plane. "Frozen stiff. Yeh, we're gonna die here."

Diana had been awakened when Urbano had moved from beneath the heap of covers. Now, both she and Casey struggled to their feet.

Diana said, "No, we won't die. I'm not going to come through a crash like this and then give up. They'll find us. They'll have all kinds of planes out looking for us. It's only a matter of time."

Urbano blew smoke from his cigarette. "Yeh, well I can only stand so much time, see? What about somethin' to eat. We'll starve to death. What the hell kinda deal is this, anyway? I knew I should have never left Chicago. It's safe there. This place will kill you."

Diana shrugged and gathered the blankets together.

Casey stood looking from Urbano to Diana, and then she spoke. "He's right. I didn't hear any planes last night and I don't hear any now. What about food? How do we know anyone is looking for us?"

Diana continued to fold the blankets. "They're looking. It's standard procedure. If Sam got our position out over the radio, they'll be here soon." She looked out through the gape in the side of the airplane. "As for food. It's out there."

Urbano took a drag on his cigarette and looked back outside. "Jesus. You sound like that guy that use to be on TV. `Food's all around us." Well, I ain't eatin' no tree bark, see? I ain't that hungry." He flipped the cigarette butt out through the hole.

Diana looked at him for a moment, and then threw a folded blanket on the growing pile. "You're not that hungry yet. But in time, you'll change your tune."

"Fat chance."

Diana moved past him and went to the exit doorway. She jumped out of the plane into the snow. The boots she wore for the flight and the wool skirt of her uniform were of little warmth in the frigid cold outside the craft. She trembled for a second, but battled her way to the baggage compartment door. She grabbed the handle and jerked on it, but it would not budge. It was frozen.

Urbano and Casey stuck their heads out of the gaping hole to see what she was doing.

Diana called to them. "Come on. Help me get this door open. I can't reach the baggage from the inside access. Both of you need warmer clothes."

They hesitated, but then both jumped out into the snow. Urbano tugged and jerked on the handle. "Damn lousy door." He kicked at it and it popped open.

Diana reached inside and pulled out a suitcase. She laid it in the snow and opened it. The case was full of a child's clothing. She carefully closed it and set it aside. Casey had pulled out another suitcase and opened it to discover men's clothing. Diana looked at it. "That's a good one. Urbano, throw that inside near the blankets."

He took the suitcase and threw it into the plane.

Casey continued to pull other pieces of luggage from the compartment, while Diana opened them. Casey spoke, "I assume you're looking for any kind of warm clothing."

"Yes," Diana answered as she pulled a sweater from one case and handed it to Urbano.

He took it and threw it inside with the other warm clothing.

"Ain't this lootin'?" He lit a cigarette. "Chicago cops would shoot you for this. Back in '67, when I was just a kid, one nearly shot my ass off." He blew smoke.

Diana and Casey stopped looking in the suitcases and turned to stare at him.

"I ain't kiddin'...Remember all the hassle back then?"

They just stared at him.

He continued. "We were taking TV's out of a store that didn't have no plate glass windows left on account of the riot..." He smiled. "I was just steppin' through the window when a cop comes round the corner and says, `Hey, drop that or I'll blow your brains out.'"

Casey was drawn in. "My God. What did you do?"

Urbano tilted his head back and blew smoke. "Me? I ain't stupid. I'm not about to throw down no TV, so I just run like hell. All of a sudden I hears this terrible bang behind me and I feels the breeze. Jesus, the dumb cop shoots me in the ass, and him talkin' about blowin' my brains out."

Diana is amused. He looked at her and winked. He took a drag on his cigarette. "You wanna see my scar?"

"No. I think I can live without seeing that." She returned to the luggage.

Casey asked, "Did you get away with the TV?"

"Hell, no. I round a corner and runs smack into another cop. He put the clamps on me fast. I spent the night in the slammer nursin' a grazed behind." He was silent for a moment. Then, he flipped the cigarette butt into the snow. "Aw, that was kid stuff. I don't do that no more. Me and my family got a restaurant. I'm a legitimate business man now." He smiled proudly.

Diana stopped looking in the cases and turned her gaze toward a knoll in the distance. "Quiet. Look over there." She pointed.

Urbano and Casey looked toward the knoll. A large buck with a huge rack stood on the rise and gazed toward them.

"Jesus," said Urbano. "Look at that. Man those horns could tear you up, huh?"

"Too bad we don't have a gun. He'd make useful food for us."

Urbano looked at Diana. "What? You crazy? You mean eat somethin' like that? Not me. I could never serve nothin' like that in my cafe." He turned to Casey. "Hey, you ever eat somethin' like that?"

"No, I never have." Casey stared at the deer and then she said to Diana. "What about food? Is there anything to eat?" The cold air made her shiver.

Diana noticed the shiver. She wanted to reach out and touch the fragile looking woman, but she didn't. "You'd better get back inside. There are a few things in the galley. As soon as I get together some different clothes, I'll see what there is."

She smiled at Urbano. "Wish we had something for you to cook. We could stand a good hot meal."

Urbano managed a smile before a gust of frigid air blasted them. He shivered.

Diana said, "Both of you should get inside and put on anything you can to keep warm.

Casey nodded.

Urbano helped her get into the airplane and he crawled in behind her. Once inside the plane, they saw the bodies again and in a macabre way found it hard to keep from looking at them. They busied themselves with the suitcases and clothing that had been thrown in a pile near the blankets.

Casey found a pair of wool slacks and with no thought of modesty, quickly removed her thin, torn skirt. The slacks were too large for her small frame, but she did not care. They would be warmer than what she had worn during the night. Her own stockings and boots were not made for this cold. She rooted around in other suitcases in search of heavier socks and found several pair. "Thank, God. My feet are freezing."

Urbano looked at her. "You'll never get your boots on over those socks."

Casey removed her boots and stockings. Her feet were pale. The toes more white than pink. She rubbed them. "Ow. Oh, they hurt."

Diana crawled into the plane. She looked at Casey's feet. "Get those socks on quickly. I found these boots in a bag. They might be too big, but they'll protect your feet." She handed Casey some heavy rubber soled boots that had leather tops and a felt lining inside.

"Thanks. My feet are freezing."

Urbano removed his top coat and pulled a tan sweater over his head. He rubbed his hands together and blew on them. "You find any gloves?" He put his coat back on.

"Yeh. Try some of these." Diana handed him several pairs of gloves. "We need a fire. Why don't you two go get some wood? Pieces of brush. Anything you can find. I'll change quickly."

Urbano pulled a pair of gloves on and stood looking in the direction of the knoll. The deer moved away into the brush.

Casey bundled herself into the boots, pulled a black plaid wool jacket over her head and tied a red scarf around her head. The gloves she wore were too large for her hands, but at least they offered some protection. "I don't know how much help I'll be. I'm not used to this."

"Shit, who is, man?" Urbano's fear blended into anger.

Diana extracted long underwear and brown corduroy pants from her flight bag. "Look, I know this isn't easy, but we have to rely on one another until help comes. Just try to find some wood. Okay?" She began to remove her skirt.

Casey looked at her, then to Urbano. "Come on. Help me."

She jumped out of the plane and struggled through the knee-deep snow toward some broken branches.

Reluctantly, Urbano followed her. "You think there's bears and stuff like that around here?"

Casey handed him some broken branches. "Probably, but what's the difference?"

He frowned. "I don't like it. When in the hell are they goin' to come and get us? They had all night. Jesus, all them animals runnin' around."

Casey moved toward other branches and jerked them from beneath the snow. Urbano seemed rooted. He did not move. She looked back at him. "Urbano, come on. Forget about animals and help me get some wood for a fire."

He walked toward her, but kept a careful eye all around him. "Why in the hell are we worrin' about a fire?"

By now, Casey was becoming angry. "It's cold. Haven't you noticed?"

"Hey, I got feelin's." He half pleaded. "Forget the sticks, lady. Let's just split."

Casey continued to gather wood. "She said we should stay with the plane."

Urbano laid his wood down and lit a cigarette. "Jeez. We stayed with that pile of junk all night and no body came, see. And I ain't heard no planes yet. That woman doesn't know what she's talkin' about."

"Think a minute. Where are you going to go?" She threw her wood into a pile.

Urbano studied her for a moment. "This is stupid. We're goin' to die here, if we don't get out by ourselves. I'm tellin' you lady, there ain't nobody lookin' for us."

Casey was angered. "You think I want to be here? I have a million dollar client waiting for me in Duluth. That's all I can think about. Dammit, I'm no good out here. I'm scared. But what chance would we have if we left the plane? You tell me."

"Hey, I'm sort of scared too. But, look, we can handle it. I've seen my share of hard times, but I survived. I've got a wife, kids, and a business now. I got reasons to live. Let's just cut out." He pleaded, "We can't be far from people…cars…apartments. Maybe even Duluth."

Casey looked at him and then looked back toward the plane. "We can't just leave. What about Diana?"

"Her? Oh, sure. We'll just tell her that we decided to walk out." He finished his cigarette and threw the remains into the snow. "If she wants to come, fine. If not, then we leave without her. It's that simple."

Casey studied his face. "I'm not so sure it's that simple."

Urbano smiled. "Sure it is. Like I told you, I got reasons to live. Nothing can stop me from getting home. Go with me. We can make it. Just trust me."

She studied his face for a few seconds and then picked up a pile of branches. "Come on. Let's take this back to the plane."

As they approached the craft, Diana stuck her head out of the gaping hole in the side of the plane. "I've found instant coffee and a metal pot. It's beat up, but I think it will work."

She jumped down to the ground and they saw that she had changed into warm clothing. She had put on several men's sweaters and had wrapped a blue wool scarf around her neck. Her curly dark hair was almost covered by a navy blue knit watch cap. On her feet she wore heavy brown leather lumberman's boots. Her blue eyes sparkled as she smiled at Casey.

Casey stared back at her. For a moment, the eye contact with Diana caused an unexplainable rush of warmth through her body, but it passed. "Coffee sounds great. Want this wood anywhere particular?"

"Just put it over there near those pine trees. They'll give us some protection."

Casey walked to an area about fifteen yards to the left and slightly toward the front of the downed plane. Snow continued to fall heavily, and although the wind was not blowing, Casey understood why Diana chose that spot. Several large spruce trees formed a wind block. Urbano followed close behind her.

"We'll just tell her we're leaving."

Casey whispered, "Just hold off a moment." She threw her wood down. She turned around to see where Diana was, and saw that she was still back at the plane wrapping something in one of the thin blankets. She yelled to Diana. "I am hungry."

Urbano threw his branches on the ground. He said nothing. He pulled off his gloves, cupped his hands and blew warm air into them. He eyed Diana with suspicion.

Diana walked over to them and placed the blanket on top of the wood. She knelt down and pushed snow away from an area that was not as deep with snow as other areas. Casey and Urbano watched.

Diana said, "I found some chocolate bars and some crackers." She looked up and smiled at them. "Some breakfast, huh?"

Urbano spoke with anger in his voice. "That's a hell of a meal!"

Diana was stung. "Look Urbano, we should be thankful for being alive. I'd like bacon and eggs for breakfast myself, but this is it." She opened the blanket and revealed a clear plastic packet that contained cellophane wrapped crackers, pretzels and candy bars. She continued, "Even at that, we're going to have to ration it." She knelt down to stack the branches for a fire.

It took a moment for Diana's words to register in Urbano's mind. Once they did, he was enraged. He got down on his knees and put his face within inches of hers. "What do you mean ration it out? Why should we?"

Diana responded. "What do you want to do? Eat it all at once and then have none left for…"

He interrupted her. "For when? Tomorrow?" He jumped to his feet and pointed his finger at Casey. "See, I knew nobody was lookin' for us. I am right. We should get out now."

Casey looked from Urbano to Diana. "Maybe he is right. I have to get to Duluth. Maybe there isn't anyone looking for us. We can't last here in this weather."

Urbano smiled. "Right lady."

Diana stopped stacking the broken twigs and wood and stood up to face them. "We have to stay with the plane. We've got to give the search party a chance. They'll have hundreds of people looking for us. Trust me."

Urbano had lit a cigarette and now, he blew smoke contemptuously. "That's what you say. What makes you an expert? I ain't heard or seen nothin' except for animals. I say we leave now." He stamped his cold feet to try to warm them.

Diana knelt back down to the wood and arranged it so that it would light with one match. She spoke as she held the match to some pine needles and small twigs. "Okay, so leave. Where do you think you're going and how far do you think you'll get in this snow?"

The twigs caught fire and the flames licked at larger pieces of wood. The smoke from the damp needles wafted skyward.

Urbano was determined. "Look here, sister. I ain't no dummy and I ain't no friggin' sissy, see? I figure we can't be too far from a town. Hell, I walked plenty far in Chicago in the winter."

Diana held her hands over the fire to warm them. "Yes, and you were never too far from a taxi or a building. This is different." She looked him squarely in the eyes.

He would not allow dissuasion and so, he turned from her gaze to Casey. "I'm tellin' ya. I know I can make it. I ain't stayin'. You with me lady?"

Casey moved closer to the fire. She put her bare hands over the ascending heat from the flames. "Urbano, look. Feel the warmth. Maybe we should stay here."

"You sidin' with her? What's the matter with you? Shit. You ain't got no million dollar client in Duluth or you'd be runnin' up that hill to find help." He took a final drag on his cigarette and flipped it into the fire.

The mention of Casey's client and the thought of a lost sale struck deep. She looked from him to Diana. "He could be right. Maybe we are just wasting our time waiting here."

Diana stood up. "All my training says, wait. Sam would have radioed our position. I don't know why we haven't seen any planes." She looked skyward, but the dense snowfall made the gesture futile. Snow covered her face. She brushed it off and looked back at them. "They have to be out there searching. Don't you see? We should give them a chance."

"Dammit. I gave 'em a chance. They had all last night and this morning. I should've left at dawn. I'd probably be in a warm place right now, eating a steak and drinking a beer, instead of arguing with a woman." He walked a little ways away from them and then turned back to Casey. "I'm leavin'. You with me?"

Casey looked at Diana.

Diana stood warming her hands over the fire. She did not want the woman to leave, but she said nothing.

Casey put her gloves back on and pulled her scarf over her ears. "All right, Urbano. I'll go with you." She said to Diana. "Come on, go with us."

Diana remained silent.

Urbano walked further away from the fire. "Come on, lady. She had her chance. Let's go."

Casey pleaded with her violet eyes. "Diana, please go with us. Don't be stubborn."

"I'm not being stubborn. I know how this weather can sneak up on you. You're not used to this. You're used to State Street."

"Don't you understand? I have to get to Duluth. If I lose that client, I lose my career."

"Think about losing your toes on your way to Duluth. And in this climate, that could happen. And probably more."

Casey looked at her feet. "What do you mean?"

"Your toes will start to burn like they're on fire and then they'll go numb. You'll stumble and when you first fall in the snow, it'll be cold. But you'll rest there and then it won't seem cold, just peaceful. You'll fall asleep and in a few hours you'll just drift into forever."

Casey looked at Diana's face and knew she meant every word. She was afraid to go, but feared more the staying. "Can you say for sure that someone will come for us?" Her violet eyes begged for assurance.

Urbano had reached the foot of the knoll and he yelled back. "Come on lady. Shelter and warmth are just over the hill." He started up the incline.

Diana broke eye contact with Casey and stared after Urbano.

"There are no assurances about anything, Casey. Except death. Even love and warmth are fleeting just like the seasons of our life." She looked back into Casey's eyes. Their gazes locked together for a brief moment.

Casey looked toward Urbano, then back at Diana. "Bye. We'll get help. There have to be people near here. We'll be back. I promise."

Diana watched Casey slog through the snow and start up the incline. Urbano had stopped at the top and stood waiting for Casey to catch up to him. Once at the top, Diana saw that Casey turned and looked back down toward the crash scene. And then, she and Urbano continued walking and very quickly disappeared into the forest amid the snowfall.

Diana was left alone. She shivered as flakes of snow stuck to her eyelashes and nose. She picked up more wood and threw it on the blaze. The flames snapped and sizzled under the deluge of white flakes that threatened to kill everything, including the fire. She stared into the flames and began to recognize her own mortality. All she had wanted this coming spring was to begin a new life with a true and lasting love. The plane crash and this place were obstacles. The fire crackled and broke her thoughts. Diana knew that she could not let herself feel the depths of loneliness and the hopelessness of defeat. From her father, who was a forest ranger, she had learned that survival depended on directed activity. She understood instinctively that the activity required of her was to make some sort of shelter away from the death inside the plane. She remembered that a compartment area in the cockpit held an emergency kit and a hand axe. It was the thought of the hand axe that stirred her imagination. Suddenly, the fear that had overcome her only moments ago, melted like the snow which touched the fire.

She plowed back through the snow to the plane intent on retrieving the hand axe. With it, she knew she could survive. She would survive. Nothing could make her give up. Nothing.

CHAPTER 5

Urbano struggled to wade through the drifts that circled the sides of the spruce trees in the forest. Sweat ran down his forehead, but he was oddly cold; in fact, chilled. He plunged forward, not knowing where he was going; only hoping that he would hear the sound of civilization. But there were no familiar sounds except the labored breathing from his burning lungs.

Casey called to him. "Wait, Urbano. I can't keep up."

Urbano turned slightly to look back for the woman and in doing so, he stumbled and fell. He staggered to his feet and stopped moving forward. He turned to face her. "Come on. We can't keep stopping. We have to find someone."

Casey was twenty-five yards behind him. She moved as fast as she could, but exhaustion had taken its toll on her.

Urbano lit a cigarette as she came up to him. "The woman was nuts to stay. I got half a mind not to tell anybody where she is." He blew smoke out of his mouth and nostrils. He coughed and rubbed his hand across his runny nose. "Come on." He began stumbling through the snow once again.

The wind had increased in velocity and the snow was no longer floating straight down as it had earlier. The fir trees blocked some of the snowfall, but the wind pushed the cold snow in swirls so fine that films of seeming ice encrusted bare skin on both Casey and Urbano. Their faces were red. Urbano's bare ears were red except for the tips which had turned white.

Casey could hardly see ahead in the fine blowing snow. She stopped and stamped her feet. They were tingling. She yelled to Urbano. "Hold up a second. My feet burn."

He stopped again and turned back to her. "Shit, my toes was burnin' for twenty minutes, but they don't hurt no more. Keep walkin', they'll be all right." He moved ahead again, but with a slower pace. "Can you imagine them pioneers puttin' up with this? Jesus, they must have been goofy. Who'd want to live out here?"

"Did you say your toes don't hurt anymore?"

"Yeh. Like they were on fire, but no more." He blew smoke and it drifted back into Casey's face. She coughed.

"Urbano, that's no good."

"Hey, the cigarette is good to me."

"I don't mean that. Your feet not hurting. That's not good."

He took a drag on his cigarette. "Feels good to me."

"Your feet are freezing. We better go back. It's like she said it would be."

Urbano looked back at Casey. "Get a hold of yourself. You sound like a frightened old lady." He flipped the remains of the cigarette into a snowdrift. "I ain't goin' back, see?" He turned and moved forward.

Casey stopped walking. She yelled to him, "I'm telling you, we'd better go back. There's nothing out here but death."

He turned back angry. "Goddammit. Don't you understand English? I ain't goin' back. There's nothin' but death back there. You can go back if you want to, but you'll go alone." He stared at her. When he saw that she did not move toward him, he turned away from her and struggled forward through drifts.

"Urbano, Urbano. I'm going back."

He yelled over his shoulder as he kept moving ahead. "So go back then. Both of you are goin' to die in this God forsaken place. Not me. I'm gettin' the hell out. I'm going back to my family." He stumbled, but kept moving away from Casey.

She stared at the dark disappearing figure. Billows of snow blew in all directions. She was frightened, but the fear of death made her turn back toward the plane. She could barely see the footprints in the snow as she tried to retrace her steps, for the falling snow was covering the path that she and Urbano had made. Casey stumbled and fell. It felt good to her. She said out loud to herself. "Get up Casey. Get up. You have to get to Duluth."

CHAPTER 6

The large amount of snow that fell in the wilds of Wisconsin was matched by an equally voluminous amount of snow that fell on Reed City in the state of Michigan. It had been snowing there for three straight days and for most people who lived in northern Michigan there was not much else to do during such a storm, but stay inside and try to keep warm.

Martin Forrester, a man in his mid fifties, who had just retired the past summer from twenty-five years service as a state game warden, found refuge in his log cabin. He had built a roaring fire in the stone fireplace right after his noon meal. The radiating heat had made him drowsy, but try as he might, he could not keep his eyes open. He lay down on the plaid sofa and pulled a navy blue throw over his lap. In no time he was asleep.

The blazing fire crackled and snapped as the aroma of pine and red oak from the burning logs permeated the cabin. The glow from the flames made the room look even cozier. Two brown leather wing back chairs were to the left of the sofa in a small circle and between them was a hand made wooden table. On the hardwood floor in front of the chairs was a thick brown and grey braided rug. A gun cabinet, full of shotguns and deer rifles, stood to the left of the fireplace. Above the mantel, a mounted thirty-five pound Chinook salmon was arched in a seeming leap. Several heavily dog-eared sports magazines laid on the coffee table by the sofa. A small wooden clock sat on an end table to the right of the mantel. Its hands read 3:15. The tranquility of the scene was shattered by the ringing of a phone on the coffee table.

Martin snapped awake. He sat up and grabbed at the phone.

"Hello, Forrester, here."

"Is this Martin Forrester?"

"Speaking."

"This is Carl Drake. I own Drake Commuter Airlines."

Martin knew instantly that something was wrong. He ran his left hand through his thick dark hair, trying to shake the sleep from his mind. "What the hell is the matter? Is something wrong with Diana?"

On the other end, Carl Drake paced nervously, not knowing exactly what to say. He said, "There's…there's been a problem."

Martin swung his kaki-covered legs off the sofa. His logging boots thumped on the floor. "What kind of problem."

"The flight Diana was on went down last night." He quickly added. "Now don't panic."

Martin's face reddened. "Don't panic? Well, where is she? Is she okay? What happened?"

"We don't know exactly what happened. We think they went down somewhere north of Eau Claire, Wisconsin, but right now, we don't have a fix on the crash site."

Martin struggled to control his fright. "What the hell are you saying? How can you not have a fix on the crash site?" He stood up and threw the cover on the sofa.

Carl sounded defensive. "Look, I know it sounds crazy, but we lost radio contact with them and we don't know where the craft went down. We sort of have an idea, but the weather is preventing any air search."

"You mean to tell me that the transponder wasn't working while they were in flight?"

"Yes, it was working, but then it cut out and…"

Martin cut him off, "Goddamit, man. What about the emergency locator transmitter? Don't tell me that wasn't working?" Martin began to pace the floor.

Carl tried to diminish the loss. "So far we haven't gotten any signal from the ELT. But, that doesn't mean that it isn't working. The weather has slowed everything down."

There was something about the way that Carl related the information that made Martin suspicious of the story he was hearing. He pressed. "You better come up with that aircraft soon. I'll be in Chicago pretty damn quick and I'm going to want some answers."

"Hey, I'm as anxious as you to locate it."

"I'll tell you one thing. Diana won't go down easy. She'll fight."

Carl was silent for a moment. "I don't know what to say…We'll find it soon. I'm sure we will."

"You damn well better be right. Good-bye, Drake. I'll see you soon." Martin did not wait for a reply, he hung up the phone. The call had drained him. He sat down on the sofa and aimlessly rolled up the sleeves on his red wool shirt to expose the thermal undershirt sleeves beneath. He put his head down and cupped it in his hands and stayed that way for several minutes. Finally, he raised his head and wiped his eyes and nose with his thermal sleeves. He glanced out the front cabin window and saw that the snow fell so thick that it looked foggy outside. He shook his head in disbelief. A log snapped and crackled in the fireplace. The noise made him stop thinking for a moment and he got up from the sofa and went to the fireplace.

He spoke out loud the words his father had taught him and the words he had taught Diana. "Directed activity. That's what this calls for. No time to muse. Directed activity." He picked up a bucket of sand that sat in front of the gun cabinet and threw it on the fire. A small cloud of smoke drifted into the room and then the chimney drafted it outside.

Martin walked into the bedroom just off the living room area to the right of the fireplace. He went to the closet and took a duffel bag off the shelf and put it on the large quilt covered bed. He returned to the closet and began to pick and choose wool shirts and pants to put in the duffel. Next, he opened the top dresser drawer and extracted underwear and socks which he stuffed into the bag on top of his shirts and pants. Finally, he put his overnight case, which contained his toiletries, on top and then he zippered the bag shut.

Martin picked up the bag and took a last look around. His eyes saw the small framed picture on his dresser and he put the bag back on the bed. He took the picture in his hands and moved closer to the bedroom window, knowing that the light from outside would cast an even illumination on the photo. He smiled at the images of himself in his thirties and of Diana in her teens. They were standing by a lake, with a canoe and camping gear behind them. So long ago.

He rubbed his thumb over the image of Diana, as if to caress a fear away. He said out loud, "You'll make it, baby. You have to. You're all I have left."

He set the framed photo back on the dresser and picked up his duffel bag. He paused long enough at the fireplace to make sure the fire was out and then, he went outside and made his way to a Jeep that was parked under a white pine next to the cabin. He threw the duffel into the back seat and hurriedly brushed the cold light snow off the windshield, then climbed inside the vehicle. The engine turned over immediately. The gears meshed into reverse and then into drive. Reed City was almost a lifetime away from Chicago and the wilds of Wisconsin, but Martin Forrester was on a mission and nothing would stop him. Snow blew skyward as the red Cherokee *Jeep* disappeared into the distance down a long and lonely dirt road.

CHAPTER 7

Since Casey and Urbano had been gone, Diana had not wasted a moment. It had been difficult for her to go back inside the plane, because of her revulsion at seeing the carnage again, but the determination to survive outweighed her anxiety. In some ways, the scene inside the plane had taken on a surreal image. The bodies had frozen during the night and the whiteness of the frozen flesh made death seem unreal. Sam and Randy were there; friends frozen in time. It reminded her of the childhood game of `Simon says', only the `Simon says, Wake up' would not work this time. She wished it could. Diana tried not to look at them as she retrieved the hand axe and the emergency medical kit from the compartment just behind Sam's seat.

As she moved back through the passenger area, she thought of other things that might come in handy. She checked each passenger for belts and shoelaces. When she found them, she took time to remove those items and place them in a knap sack she had found in an overhead bin. The task had not been easy, but again, the thought of her survival made her set aside any thought of not taking what might be useful to her. Those frozen images would not miss what she took. They were beyond all earthly hurts or slights. The sorrow would be left for the living.

Somewhere from outside the plane came the mournful cry of an animal. Diana stopped what she was doing and listened. The cry came again. She recognized the wail of a wolf. She went to the hole in the side of the plane and looked outside. A lone wolf stood atop a craggy rock on a ridge about a hundred yards straight out from the left side of the aircraft. It howled once more and turned toward the safety of the pine forest and loped away from her view.

She jumped down from the plane and made her way back to the fire, carrying blankets, several seat cushions, the hand axe and the knapsack. She surveyed the area near the fire and decided to move further away from the plane toward some spruce and white pine trees near the foot of the small hill where she had seen the wolf. The site would offer more protection from wind. The craggy rock would also act as a landmark, should she have time to explore her surroundings.

Diana put the cushions, blankets and knapsack under a pine tree and began to chop lower limbs off the trees. The hand axe was sharper than she thought it would be and she was thankful for that. When she had chopped and gathered a dozen or more branches, she fashioned a lean-to shelter and a fire windbreak in front of the fire pit she dug in the snow. Her efforts took on a mission of desperation. She labored steadily and with designed purpose.

As she worked, she thought back to the forests of Michigan and the lessons that her father had taught her. How strange it was to think that those camping trips were exercises in survival. She spoke out loud, "You'd be proud, Dad." She paused a moment to look around at the wilderness and then added, "And, I am grateful."

Her efforts took several hours and finally she was done. The lean-to faced toward the plane. The pine boughs were sturdy and easy to work into the snow and to fashion into a roof. She had placed the seat cushions on the floor of the shelter and piled the blankets on them. The blankets served two purposes; some to cover up with and two she used to place over the top of the shelter. She utilized shoelaces to tie those blankets in place and once done, they made the roof somewhat impervious to wind. She knew she could survive now. Her shelter was done.

The windbreak she had made for the fire pit had taken longer because she could not use pine boughs. They were not sturdy enough for that. Diana had taken the time to search out small birch and pine trees. She chopped them down and stripped off all limbs, so that only trunks measuring six feet in length were left. When she had finished half a dozen of them, she stacked them into a wall between the upright posts she had jammed into the snow. She packed snow behind the wall to give it further stability. She was satisfied that it would serve its purpose of reflecting heat toward the shelter and prevent heavy wind from blowing glowing fire ashes onto the blankets inside her lean-to.

All of this effort had taken several hours and she was tired. She gathered wood and smaller branches and twigs to make a fire. She was done for now and all she could think about was warmth and a cup of coffee. She lit the fire and as it grew in size, added more wood. From the knapsack, she extracted the small metal pot she had found among the wreckage and packed it with clean snow. She placed it near the flames and while she waited for the snow to melt, Diana emptied a packet of instant coffee and put some pine needles into a cup.

The wind had picked up some, but now the snow was not falling as heavily. Diana looked toward the hill that Urbano and Casey had climbed earlier in the morning and she wondered where they were and how they were doing. She suddenly felt very alone. The woman with the violet eyes reminded her of someone she had once loved. Diana wanted to find someone to share her life with forever. Just get lost in the other, but she had been alone for years. Casey might be someone to get lost with, but Casey was gone. Diana poured the steaming water from the small pot into her cup and watched the granules of coffee dissolve and the pine needles float and swirl in the steam. She became lost in thought.

CHAPTER 8

In another part of the woods, Casey stumbled and fell against a tree. She leaned on it, her eyes looked downward in the snow, searching for the path that she and Urbano had made. Here and there, traces of their movement through the snow could be seen and she had relentlessly followed the path backward. The wind constantly threatened to cover the way, but she would not give up.

She stood there for a moment and then catching sight of a seeming pathway, she moved ahead. Her pace was slow, for she was tired. She stumbled again and there was no tree to stop her fall. She lie in the snow and shut her eyes. Her mind did not stop and in it she heard the words of Diana.

"...you'll rest there and then it won't seem cold, just peaceful. You'll fall asleep and in a few hours, you'll drift into forever." The words echoed in her head. They would not stop. Casey shook her head violently from side to side and with all her strength, made herself get up. She rubbed snow on her closed eyes.

She moved forward. "I can't die here. Oh, God. I can't."

Ahead of her she could see the ground drop and a distant ridge of pine trees and spruce. The smell of smoke drifted toward her and her eyes opened wide. She could feel the adrenaline flow through her. If only she could get to the rim of the hill ahead, she knew that she had a chance of getting back to the crash site.

The drifts impeded her progress and the sudden burst of energy that she had experienced only moments ago, faded. She stumbled. So close. So close. Casey saw the rim's edge and staggered and stumbled down. She crawled and clawed her way toward it. She could see the smoke now and she yelled and howled for help. She struggled to her feet and let out a sound more animal than human. Then she pitched forward on the hill and rolled and tumbled downward.

At first, the sound that Diana heard made no sense to her. She thought she had imagined it. She looked toward the plane and then a second wail directed her attention toward the hill. Through the falling snow, she caught sight of a human figure at the top of the hill to her left, the way that Casey and Urbano had gone. She jumped to her feet. There was another pitiful cry from the figure before it stumbled and pitched down the embankment. She ran toward the hill, not knowing if it was Casey or Urbano or someone else. All she knew was that someone needed her and she knew by then that she needed someone else to ease her sense of isolation.

As Diana came nearer the figure which lay face down in the snow, she saw the red scarf and black plaid jacket and knew that it was Casey. Her heart beat wildly. She knelt down and lifted Casey's head.

In a weak voice Casey spoke. "I'm cold. My feet are numb. I want to sleep. Help me. Help me."

"It's going to be okay, but you have to get up." Diana struggled to get the limp body in an upright position.

"I can't. I just want to sleep."

"Come on, Casey. Help me. I can't drag you or carry you through this snow. You have to do some of this yourself." Diana wrapped her arms around Casey's upper torso and managed to lift her upright against her body. She could smell the perfume from her hair. She mentally blocked out the scent.

"I can't walk. I can't make my feet work."

"You have to. I'll help all I can. Lean on me, Casey. The fire is warm and close. Just a little ways off."

The mention of a fire sparked Casey's hopes and she tried to move her legs. Diana steadied her. "I can't feel what I'm doing. It's like my legs and feet are not part of me."

Diana circled Casey's waist with her right arm and pulled her left arm over her shoulder and braced the woman. "Don't think about that. Just concentrate on putting one foot in front of the other. Your legs will do what they're supposed to do." She was half carrying Casey.

The movement toward the shelter was slow and deliberate. The snow blew into their faces and made the struggle all the harder, but Diana was determined.

"I just want to lie down. Just let me go."

"Dammit, Casey, screw up your courage. You're suffering from hypothermia. I can't let you go. We'll get there. Just keep walking."

Casey went limp and dropped to her knees, pulling Diana down with her. Diana felt like she was fighting a drowning victim. She was angry. "Get up. You have to get up." She pulled back Casey's eyelid and saw that the woman had passed out. Her anger left and fright took over. She grabbed the collar of Casey's jacket and began pulling and dragging the woman toward the shelter. She would take two short steps and then pull hard to move the dead weight a few feet at a time toward warmth and safety. The lean-to was only a couple of hundred yards away, but it seemed as though it was miles.

Above the campsite, atop the craggy out jutting rock on the ridge of the hill, two wolves stood and watched the struggle below. The male raised its head and howled into the wilderness. The falling snow blanketed his back and that of his mate. The smaller female nuzzled his ear as if to speak of something private. He did not howl again.

Diana heard the sound and saw them. She stopped for a moment and stared. She knew the wolves would not hurt them; that they were only curious.

She moved forward again and thought of her father. "I'm trying, Dad. I'm trying to take care of me." And then she added. "And another." She pulled and tugged and dragged. Stumbled and fell. Got up and pulled and tugged and dragged some more. She would not give up. It was not in her nature to quit.

She was closing in on the shelter. It was now only twenty-five yards away and the closeness of it, gave her added energy. She felt a sense of winning. Just as she reached the lean-to, the wolf gave a final howl and Diana smiled. She looked up, but the trees blocked her vision and she could not see the fan who had howled approval.

Diana pulled Casey inside the small walls and slanted roof of the shelter and onto the cushions. Casey moaned. Diana pushed her as far to the back as she could and then piled all the blankets she had on top of Casey.

Then she turned to the fire, where she had left the metal pot and put more snow into it. In a short time the snow melted. Water in the pot sent vapors of steam into the afternoon air. Diana rummaged in the knapsack and found some packets of sugar which she emptied into a cup, along with a tea bag and some of the steaming water. She returned to Casey.

Diana lifted Casey's head and saw the eyelids flutter. It was a good sign. "Here, drink some of this. It will warm you."

Casey opened her eyes. She drank slowly from the cup. She spoke. "Oh, Diana, my feet hurt. Burn."

"I have to take your boots off. Drink a little more tea and then lie back down."

She helped Casey finish the tea and then took the cup and placed it back near the fire. Casey lay still while Diana began to remove her boots. She pulled the socks off and flinched when she saw the pale white toes. She looked at Casey's face and saw that she was biting her lip as though in pain.

Casey asked, "Well?"

"I'm going to have to do something to try to get your toes to pink up again. Just trust me." Diana threw several large pieces of wood on the fire and then moved inside the shelter and took a position at the base of Casey's feet. She pulled the exposed feet into her lap and put them up inside her sweater onto her bare stomach and then jerked her sweater over the feet and drew her coat tight. She put sections of blankets around herself and over the legs of Casey. "Does that feel better?"

Casey did not answer; she had fallen asleep.

Diana studied the face of the woman who slept next to her. The bump on the head suffered in the initial crash had diminished some. The light brown eyelashes that shaded her violet eyes were clamped shut in sleep. Diana thought the woman was beautiful. She wondered what the woman would think if she knew that Diana was becoming interested in knowing her, knowing everything about her. Would she be offended? This was no woman that frequented bars looking for love. Casey seemed centered, caring; someone a person could love above all others. Maybe that "someone" Diana had spent her life looking for but had never found. Diana looked away from Casey and stared into the fire.

Dusk came then. The fire blazed brightly. Snow began to fall heavier and the wind moaned again. Swirls of snow danced by the lean-to, but inside it, Casey slept peacefully. Diana nodded and dozed off into a warm sleep.

CHAPTER 9

The twin engine USAir Express landed in a swirl of snow at Midway Airport in Chicago. The Pratt and Whitney engines whined as the aircraft rolled down the runway and then turned off onto the blue lit taxi-way and headed toward the terminal. It had been a routine flight from Saginaw to Midway and although many of the thirty passengers had slept during the evening flight, Martin Forrester had remained awake. He was anxious and edgy. He knew better, but he already had his seatbelt undone before the craft reached the terminal. He wanted out. He wanted a shot at Carl Drake. His instincts told him that there was something drastically wrong when no one could locate an aircraft as large as a Mohawk 298. This was the second night. He wanted out.

The airplane came to a smooth stop. Martin was out in the aisle and had already retrieved his duffel bag from the overhead bin. He waited. All around him the other passengers came to life and the sound of buckles snapping open and the scuffling of feet and yawns permeated the air. He moved forward.

The steward opened the exit door just aft the cockpit. The ground crew rolled out the stairway and snuggled it up to the open front exit. Martin was out into the snow before the steward had time to tell him, "Thanks for flying USAir." He walked hurriedly into the terminal and made his way into the main lobby. He looked around for something that indicated Drake Airlines, but saw nothing. He approached a counter.

"I'm trying to locate Drake Airlines."

The blond man looked up from some paper work and pointed. "Down that hallway, first door on the left." He went back to his papers.

"Thanks." Martin proceeded in the direction he was told and opened the door. The room was shabby with soiled paint and battered wooden furniture. A chubby young woman seated at the desk looked up as he entered.

"May I help you?"

"Yeh, I'm trying to locate Carl Drake. I'm Martin Forrester. Diana's father."

"Oh, yes. I'm so sorry about the accident." She stood up and moved around the desk. "We are all upset. Mr. Drake is in the flight planning room with NTSB and FAA people."

"I'll bet. Where's that?"

The woman put her hand on his shoulder and moved him back toward the doorway. "You go back into the hall and turn left. It's the second door on your right." Her brown eyes showed concern. "I am real sorry."

Martin started out the door and she called to him. "Mr. Forrester, sometime talk to Frank Rawlins."

He nodded to her and then continued back down the hallway and entered the door into the flight planning room which was well lit. It contained several large tables in the center of the room with two stacks of file drawers along the right wall. On the left wall hung an enormous map of the world. Five clocks were positioned above the map, each reading a different time. Underneath them were signs indicating the time locations: London, New York, Moscow, Sydney, and Buenos Aires.

Three men and a woman leaned on the center tables and studied a series of charts. They looked up as Martin entered.

One man spoke. "This is off limits, mister."

"I'm Martin Forrester. I'm looking for Carl Drake."

Drake rolled a cigar stub in his mouth and said, "I'm Drake."

He stuck his hand out to Martin. He turned to the others, "This is our stewardess's father."

The man who first spoke extended his hand. "Hello, I'm Bill Hutchins, NTSB. Chicago."

The red haired woman grabbed his hand and smiled. "I'm Marilyn Keane. FAA."

The last man was a tall thin slightly built man. His grey hair was sparse, but neatly combed. His tweed jacket seemed too large for his frame and he squinted from behind thick oversized glasses. He walked around the table and extended his hand. "Gene Cramer here." His firm handshake surprised Martin. "I'm search coordinator. Nice to make your acquaintance." He smiled a thin grin.

Martin thought of Woody Allen. He said, "Glad to see all of you here. You make me feel better."

Gene moved back behind the table. He cleared his throat. "At this point, Mr. Forrester, we don't have too much to go on, but we're hopeful. Drake tells us that you have quite a background in military air search and rescue."

Martin wondered how Drake knew that. Diana probably. "Yeh. I guess the Vietnam War did prepare me for some things besides fighting." He dropped his duffel onto the seat of a wooden chair underneath the wall map and moved to look at the charts on the table. "What was the craft's last known position?"

Marilyn answered, "We're not sure how accurate our information is at this point."

Martin frowned and turned to Drake.

Carl quickly jumped to his own defense. "There seemed to be some sort of radio problem early on in the flight. Even the transponder was not functioning properly. We don't know why."

Martin made a sudden move toward Carl. Cramer stepped between the two and faced Martin, diffusing the confrontation. "Right now, the best information we have is from Minneapolis Center. They believe flight Niner three's last known position was seventy five miles east Northeast of Eau Claire, Wisconsin."

Martin glared at Drake but he moved away.

Hutchins from NTSB took up the slack, "They were assigned flight path Victor 129 out of Eau Claire at about 10:45 our time. There was a radio problem then."

Martin momentarily forgot Drake and went over to the table and looked at the sectional charts. He put his finger on the flight path and looked up at Hutchins. "Seventy five miles east Northeast of Eau Claire puts them off course quite a bit."

"Yes, it does," Hutchins said.

Martin was angry now. He approached Carl. "Did you know anything about this `radio problem' prior to the flight?"

Carl's face turned red. He shifted the cigar stub around in his mouth. "Everything was working fine. We check our equipment all the time. Hell, I wouldn't let one of my ships go unless it was in top notch condition."

"You damn well better be sure the mechanic's records reflect that. They were a hell of a long ways off course, if Minneapolis is right."

Carl jerked the cigar stub out of his mouth and threw it at a trashcan. "Hey, pal. Are you trying to infer something?"

Martin reached out and grabbed Carl's necktie and pulled his face to within inches of his. "I'm not going to `infer' anything. When we find the craft, I'll let you know what I think. Get the drift?" He pushed Drake away.

Cramer poked Hutchins, who stepped in to confront Martin. "Back off. I know you're upset about your daughter. If anything wasn't right with the maintenance we'll deal with that. Right now, we've got to try to locate where it went down."

Carl moved over to the file cabinets and leaned on one. He pulled a cigar from his inside coat pocket and cut the end off with a small pocketknife he had taken from his wrinkled suit pants. He lit the *Macanudo* and watched from a distance as the others bent over the charts on the table. He adjusted his tie.

Martin asked. "What makes you figure that they may have gone down east Northeast of Eau Claire?"

Cramer responded. "Emergency radio confirmation."

"Like how?"

Cramer was all business now. He cleared his throat and said with an official tone. "The craft was a Nord Mohawk 298 with cruise ability of over 200 miles per hour. At eleven fifteen, a Mayday call was picked up by Duluth. It was heard just once. If Minneapolis radar is correct on their fix and we couple that with the Duluth Mayday call, then Niner three went down in that area."

"What makes you think the Mayday call was from the Mohawk?"

Gene was pleased with his calculations and the pride shown on his face. "Flight niner three is the only craft that could have put out that call. It's the only one missing."

Martin was placated. "Okay. So maybe you're right. What's the terrain like up there?"

Marilyn answered. "I lived in Duluth for a while and became familiar with that region. It's desolate and this kind of weather makes air search tough. In fact, maybe out of the question until the snow squalls move out of the area."

"Are there any airstrips close to where you think they went down?"

Hutchins spoke. "Yeh, there's a couple of small strips. Hayward is an Omni station and there's a pretty good runway there."

Martin turned to Cramer. "Well, Gene, you're calling the shots on the search. What's the plan?"

"All we can do is wait for the weather to break. Official agencies in the area north of Eau Claire have been looking and trying to get information, but so far, no one has reported finding anything."

Martin rubbed his right hand through his hair. He blew air between his lips. "What about civil air patrol?"

Gene thumbed through a notebook he picked up from the chart table. "There is a unit in the Hayward area. A fellow by the name of Joe Finney heads it. He's already confirmed that they'll get airborne as soon as daylight breaks......provided that the weather is half way decent."

Martin sighed. "Jesus. I think I'll rent a small airplane and head up to Hayward. I can't see hanging around here......waiting. I've got to do something. I'm going crazy."

Marilyn put her hand on Martin's shoulder. "We're bound to hear something soon. Someone has to know where it went down."

Martin nodded and blew air out again. He moved to the door and then turned back. "Thanks for everything. I know one thing. Diana's tough. I taught her to be a survivor. If she made it through the crash, she'll be okay. No matter how long it takes to find her, she'll be okay." He left.

Gene watched the door close and then turned to Carl, who still stood by the file cabinets. "Mr. Drake. This is one time you'd better pray for pilot error. I wouldn't want to face that man, if it was mechanical failure."

Carl managed a weak grin. The sweat poured off his forehead. He blew a large puff of cigar smoke and fidgeted with his tie.

"The plane was fine. Sam was sort of a hot dog pilot. You know. Took risks. Maybe it just caught up with him. Yeh...a hot dog."

The pungent cigar smoke drifted across the room in lazy waves.

The three government people poured over the charts and ignored Carl. There would be time later to deal with him, if necessary.

For now, they were intent on finding flight niner three.

CHAPTER 10

Smoke from the fire drifted skyward into the night and into the deluge of falling snow. The burnt wood smoldered with brilliant orange ambers that snapped and crackled with every frozen crystal that touched the heat. Inside the lean-to, both Casey and Diana were asleep. Diana had fallen over slightly in the opposite direction from Casey. Her gloved hand lay in a protective manner over the blankets that covered Casey's feet which were still inside Diana's jacket.

The crackling fire awakened Casey. She opened her eyes and for a moment was unsure of her surroundings. Then a puzzled look crossed her face. She looked toward Diana. "What do I feel with my toes? Flesh?"

Diana rose up on her elbow and smiled at Casey. "Yes, and I'm glad to hear that you can feel with them."

Casey's face flushed. She pulled her feet out from underneath the covers.

Diana took off her gloves and held Casey's feet in her warm hands. "Let me see." She inspected the soles and each of the toes and found them to be slightly pink. "You must lead a charmed life. You get to keep all ten of them."

Casey sat up and began to rub her feet. Diana handed her several pairs of socks, which she immediately put on.

Diana moved out of the shelter toward a small woodpile and jerked several pieces of wood from underneath the snow. She threw them on the embers. The small logs crackled and then caught fire from the intense heat of the coals. The flames illuminated the night with red and yellow dancing flames.

Casey watched her. "Thank you, Diana. I could have died. I was stupid to leave."

Diana took the metal pot and packed snow into it and placed it near the fire. "Maybe you weren't. At least not in the idea." Then she added. "And I'm glad you didn't die." She moved back into the shelter and sat down. She did not continue the dialog. She studied the fire.

"What do you mean the idea?"

"You want some coffee?" Diana moved to the pot and the melted snow. She brought it back to the shelter. "There are some packets of tea and some coffee in the knapsack just behind you." She searched around near the back of the shelter and retrieved two cups.

Casey rummaged in the knapsack. She handed Diana the coffee packets and waited while she poured the contents and then steaming water into her cup. She asked again. "What did you mean by `the idea'?"

Diana swirled her coffee around in her cup and stared at the fire. "My whole world is screwy. I thought everything would just flow along, but fate throws strange curves. I never really thought about anything like this." She pointed into the dark surroundings. "`The idea?'" She turned to face Casey. "Your idea and Urbano's. To leave this place and find help."

"What about it?"

"All my training, both in airline work and from my father says to stay, but somehow I don't think that that is the right way now. There is something that tells me that no one knows where we are and we can't stay."

"But you were so sure about staying?"

"Yeh. That was like ages ago."

"Well, this is a good shelter; we could last here for some time, couldn't we? I don't understand the change."

Diana got up and stepped toward the fire. She threw a small log on it.

"I know that I could make it because my father taught me well. He was a game warden in northern Michigan. My mom died in a canoe trip when I was about eight years old and after that, Dad took me everywhere with him and showed me how to live off the land. Vietnam taught him the art of survival and to do whatever it takes to save yourself and those around you. Some things, I wish I hadn't learned."

"What are you getting at? I don't know anything about being out here, Diana. I grew up in Oak Park and that wasn't any kind of woods. The only camping I ever did was in a trailer at a State Park in southern Michigan. My dad knew how to back the thing up and hook it to electricity. God, we had TV and everything."

"Yeh. Not like here, huh?" Diana stood staring into the fire.

"I trust you and I think we should stay. It's better here now with the shelter and all. Why the change?

"We can't stay. What about Urbano?"

"You mean we should find him?"

"No, I don't think we will, but where did he go?"

Casey sipped the last of her warm coffee. "I don't know. I hope to God he that made it. The last I saw of him, he was stumbling. I think his feet were freezing. Then he simply disappeared."

Diana sighed. "I shouldn't have been so stubborn. We needed more time to think." She paused. "I needed more time to think." The falling snow had settled on her shoulders and on top of the watch cap she wore. She shivered.

"I'm hungry, Diana. Is there anything to eat?"

Diana spun around and the snow from her cap and shoulders swirled outward. "That's what's changed. That's why we can't stay." She sounded angry.

Casey was jolted by the intensity of the remark. "I…I can't help that I'm hungry."

"I know and that's exactly why we have to leave."

"I don't understand."

Diana said with no niceties attempted. "You see that plane full of bodies?"

"Yes."

"Hunger and those bodies are why we can't stay."

"But that makes no sense to me."

"If you get hungry enough, you'll understand. They're food for us when there is nothing else."

"You mean, eat them?"

Diana loomed above Casey. "Yes."

Casey looked toward the plane. Her mouth hung open and then she chewed her lip. "I would never do that. Never."

"I've learned to never say never. My dad taught me that hunger and survival bring out all sorts of animals within us. In time, Casey, we would do whatever it takes to keep ourselves alive. And that includes eating whatever we could find and they are very close at hand."

Casey's face went white and she choked back the desire to throw up. She grabbed some snow and rubbed it across her face and mouth. "If you really believe that would happen, then I want to leave. I would never eat them, but if you did, it would make me crazy." Her violet eyes examined Diana's face.

Never flinching, Diana stared back at her, until Casey averted her gaze to the fire. Somewhere the faint cry of a wolf sounded above the snapping of the burning wood.

Casey spoke softly. "I'll go."

"I thought you would. And this time, we'll make it."

Diana would not let Casey know that she had other fears, and that those fears were not about survival of the flesh. Those fears were about survival of the heart.

The wolf cried again and the sound was lost in the fading of the night. Dawn crept upon them ever so gently. Diana stared at the early morning light. "Today marks the beginning of a new journey toward unknown vistas. We should get a little rest before we start."

CHAPTER 11

Morning light was all around them. Diana, who was standing by the fire, bent down and picked up the metal pot of heated water. She dropped a small bag into a cup in which she poured some hot water. She added a tea bag and handed the cup it to Casey.

"You can take the makeshift bag out in a few minutes."

"What's in it? It looked like you put in pine needles."

Diana was amused. "I did."

Casey studied her cup and the little bag. "What in the world for?"

"It's a dad trick. I learned it from him. Pine needles are full of vitamin C. Before this is over, we'll have to eat all sorts of things you probably never ate before."

"I'm sure." Casey removed the small bag. She sipped the tea and moved the liquid from side to side. "Not bad really. Sort of like drinking *Pine Sol.*"

Diana laughed and took a drink of her own brew. She swished it around in her mouth and laughed again. "Damn, you're right."

Casey laughed with her.

Diana looked out across the snow-covered terrain and back at the shattered remains of the aircraft. She set her cup down and picked up some blankets and began folding them into packs and fastening them with belts and shoelaces. Her mind was bristling with ideas and thoughts about going.

"Before we leave, there are two things we must do. First, we have to search through the plane again and the luggage for anything that will help us survive."

Casey winched, "Do we have to go inside?"

"Yes. Or you can wait outside and go through the baggage compartment."

Casey was relieved. "I'll do that. What's the other thing we have to do?" She finished her tea and put the cup next to her.

"We have to fashion an arrow out of pine boughs." Diana pointed to an open area toward the hill that Casey and Urbano had climbed the day before. "Over there."

"What for?"

"If anyone comes here, they'll know someone went that way. Sooner or later, they'll follow. I'll notch trees as we go."

Casey spoke. "I want you know that if this had to happen, I'm glad that you survived. I could not make it without you. I mean that."

Diana looked up from what she was doing and smiled at Casey.

Casey watched as Diana rolled and fashioned packs. Her face flushed. She stammered out, "When do we go to the plane? And, what should I look for?"

Diana threw the last pack inside the shelter. "Now. Look for anything that we could use. Knives. Socks. Gloves. Any kind of nourishment." She paused. "A deer rifle."

Casey had been attentive, but the last one threw her.

"Who would have a deer rifle?"

Diana laughed out loud. "Just kidding. Wishful thinking. You know." She looked at the plane and then at Casey. "Come on. We might as well do it." She headed through the drifts to the plane.

Casey reluctantly followed.

Diana crawled inside the cold metal remains of flight niner three. There was no avoiding contact with the frozen bodies. They seemed to be everywhere, covered in frozen pale blood. She heard Casey moving around inside the baggage compartment. Diana gritted her teeth and began the task of searching again through compartments and under seats for baggage that might contain items for their survival.

Inside the baggage compartment, Casey had very little light, just enough to see other cases and baggage that were further inside. She opened some and found socks and gloves and scarves. She pulled them out and threw them towards the doorway. Back in the corner was a thin, long box package. She crawled over to it and ripped at the taped seams. It was averse to opening, which only made Casey more determined. She pushed it toward the hatchway. "Damn." She muttered. Then she yelled. "Diana I found some kind of odd package."

Diana was still working her way through the compartment contents. "I'll be there in a minute."

Casey had the package by the opening now. She pushed the clothing out of the way. The box intrigued her. "Probably not a damn thing worth saving." She removed her gloves, dug a fingernail into the tape and ripped at it. The tape broke and so did her well-manicured nail. She stuck her finger in her mouth and sucked it. "Shit. Well, now I'll know if it was worth it."

She pulled the tape off and lifted back the cardboard top. Inside was a long thin black box. She moved toward the opening and jumped outside scattering gloves and socks behind her. She slid the thin box out onto the snow.

"What do you have?" Diana jumped down from the plane and came to where Casey stood.

"I just got it out. I don't know."

They lifted the thin box out of the cardboard container and set it down in a drift. Casey snapped the silver latch open and revealed a double bladed shiny axe.

Diana let out a scream of delight. "Oh, my God. Oh, my God. It's beautiful." She grabbed Casey and hugged her. She jumped up and down. She kissed Casey's face.

Casey blushed. "I did good, I guess."

Diana shook her head. "Good? This is a find of a lifetime. We'll make it for sure. Nothing can stop us now."

Casey looked at the double-bit axe in the case. "I don't get it. Why would that be in there? I've never seen one like it."

"It's special. Competition." Diana picked up the stainless steel axe and looked closely at the edges. "Sharp as hell."

"I still don't understand."

Diana looked at her. "This is way beyond Chicago. Up here they have lumbermen's competition. Like who can chop a tree down the fastest? Who can skin a tree the fastest? It's a real art. This axe was special ordered no doubt. The guy's going to miss it, but what the hell. It's ours now."

Casey watched as Diana turned the axe blade around and around to inspect it. She saw the delight in Diana's face. "I don't get it, but it must be important."

"You have no idea how important this really is. This is like a small miracle. Come on. Let's take our loot over to the shelter and pack it up. I have some frozen candy bars over there. We'll split one." She grabbed some of the clothing and headed toward the lean-to.

Casey smiled and followed.

CHAPTER 12

Wind blew snow devils around the small rusty colored wooden building. Yellow block letters on the front side of the building toward the parking lot read, Hayward Airport. Above the door leading from the taxi area was a small sign which proclaimed, "Elev. 1215." An Army Reserve plane dominated an area to the left of the building, while to the right stood a row of half a dozen metal hangars. They groaned and moaned in the wind, but remained secure. The runway was scraped clear of snow. Here and there patches of asphalt, dark and shiny dotted the mile long strip. A windsock snapped out straight atop the small building.

Inside, the three rooms which made up the terminal, it was warm and the smell of coffee wafted through the air. A huge wooden desk dominated the area behind a counter that was to the right as one entered from the airstrip. Various aerial charts were piled atop the desk along with a communication's radio and two phones.

Odds and ends of chairs, both plastic and wood were scattered about the room, some near the front windows and others near a table which was in the center of the main room. Overhead fluorescent lights illuminated years of cigarette burns and spilled coffee and dug in pen and pencil marks which marred the tabletop. In a small room, reserved for pilots, pieces of shirts hung on the wall above a plaid orange couch. Names and dates of solo pilots, who had had their tails clipped, were scrawled in dark ink across the material. Faded badges of honor.

Martin Forrester looked at the names. He smiled in remembering his own tail clipping so long ago. He moved to a small wooden table at the back of the room and poured himself a cup of coffee from the *Bunn* pot. The aroma was strong. He went back into the main room where two men were studying a map on a bulletin board which hung on the wall behind the desk.

"So what do you think?" Martin asked.

The short wiry one, named Joe Finney, turned from the chart to Martin who had moved to the front windows. Light red hair stuck out from beneath his green plaid wool baseball cap. "If they actually were on track out of Eau Claire, Victor 129 should have put them right across Rice Lake airport. None of the guys down there heard anything."

Martin frowned. He sipped at his coffee.

Finney continued. "Hell, the Chippewa's know that area like a beaver knows where to find birch and poplar trees. Nothin' went down there. I'm tellin' ya, something had to be screwy with their nav system."

The other man, Al Hartman, who was tall and heavyset, with a large bulbous nose and balding head, pushed up his flannel shirtsleeves. "All right, Joe. So where does that leave us?"

Joe lit a cigarette. He looked back at the chart. "I think we need to start looking north of the 46th degree latitude." He put his left index finger on the chart. "And east of the 92nd degree longitude. Forget below that."

Martin had been alternating between looking out the window at the falling snow and watching Joe and Al fuss over the charts. He turned now from the window. "How the hell can you just write off an area? Christ, nobody reports having seen or heard anything. How can that be? It's like they just dropped off the face of the earth. I'm not going to write off any area yet."

Finney flushed. "So maybe we don't write off that area. I don't think we should start there though. Believe me, Martin; the Indians in that area know what happens in their territory. We'll get reports." He took a drag on his cigarette.

Martin finished his coffee. "I know you men are doing all you can. This damn weather is frustrating. I just want to find her."

Al moved away from the chart and sat down at the desk. "I'll call flight service at Eau Claire and double check with Houghton." He chuckled to ease the tension. "Maybe they're handing out better weather this afternoon." He picked up the flight service phone and listened intently, taking notes.

Joe walked to the table and sat down. He finished his cigarette and doused it in a metal coffee can. "Why don't you relax for a while?"

Martin ran his hand through his dark hair and walked to the table. He pulled a chair out and braced his right foot on the seat. He half leaned on his bent leg. "I flew all kinds of missions in Nam and in all kinds of weather, but this has me beat. You just can't see anything. It's like flying inside a flour can. Nothin' but white out."

Joe rolled a pencil back and forth across the tabletop. "It's hard to figure why nobody hasn't spotted anything. There's sure been enough news coverage. Usually that gets some sort of response. Yep, hard to figure." He got up and went to the coffee table and poured himself some coffee.

Al finished listening to the recorded message and hung up the phone. "Out of luck Forrester. Both stations are predicting heavy snow and wind chill down to twenty-five below. It looks like this is going to keep up for another five days or so. One of those good ole Artic systems."

"Dammit." Martin was clearly shaken.

Joe asked, "Any chance at all of getting up?"

Al moved around the desk to the front of the counter. "Oh, sure. The weather could change, but it's a long shot." He leaned on the edge of the counter, facing them.

Martin had his head in his hands. Suddenly he banged his fist on the table. "Dammit all to hell. I wish I knew if she survived the impact. If only somebody would report something. Just one little thing."

Joe moved quickly to the table and set his coffee down. He went to Martin's side and put his arm on his shoulder. "Hey, pal. It'll be okay. Why don't you go back to the motel and try to relax. Get yourself a bottle of Jack Daniels or go down to the Fish Museum and look at Muskies. We'll call if we hear anything." He patted Martin's back. "There's nothing we can do now."

"I know. I know. Go back to the motel or the museum?" Martin pulled his foot off the chair and stood on both legs. He jammed his hands in his pants pockets as he paced to the window. "You're right Joe. I am tired, but there's no sleep. I could take it, if Diana didn't make it. It's worse not knowing one way or the other. I've never felt this helpless."

Al spoke. "I'll put a call into Cramer down at Chicago later today. Maybe some information went down to them and it just didn't make it back up to us. That kind of stuff happens you know."

Martin managed a weak smile. "Thanks fellows. I know you've tried."

Joe sat on the edge of the table and drank his coffee. "I wish it was different. But it isn't. Just try to relax. Think about good times. If your daughter is as tough as you say she is, then she'll make it."

Martin moved to a coat rack which was nailed to the wall in the pilot's room and got his coat. "She'll make it. I know she will. You're right about the motel. I'll go. There's nothing here for me to do. Not yet." He put his coat on and went to the door at the back of the small building. He gave a half salute to the two men. "Call, if you hear anything." Then he left.

Al and Joe watched a small amount of snow blow into the entrance as Martin left. A momentary chill permeated the warm room.

Al walked to the front windows and looked outside at the swirling snow. He turned to Joe. "What do you think?"

"About what?"

"His daughter. Or any of them for that matter."

Joe cupped both hands around his coffee mug. "Even the Chippewa's find this weather rough. Forrester is living on false hope. We're too use to civilization. I couldn't make it out there more than a few days in this weather. What about you?"

Al looked back outside. "Me neither. Hell, I hate walking the short distance between my truck and this building."

Joe lit a cigarette and rolled the smoke around in his mouth. "I know one thing," he said as he exhaled smoke.

"What?"

"If that plane went down because of any kind of mechanical problem, whoever is responsible is going to have hell to pay." He blew a large smoke ring. "Hell to pay."

Al looked back outside. The snow was so heavy he couldn't see across the runway to the trees that ran around the perimeter of the field. It was a total white out. He spoke, "It's warm inside. Nobody could survive outside for very long."

"No, I don't think so," Finney agreed.

"I'll do my job, but some things are a given. Being lost in something like this weather can have only one outcome. Death." Al turned and looked at Joe.

"C'est la vie."

"Yeh, so be it."

CHAPTER 13

Snow fell in huge flakes, as Diana knelt on a blanket inside the lean-to and inspected the items that she and Casey found in the plane and in the luggage. It was an odd assortment of packets of tea, coffee, sugar, pretzels and innumerable small bottles of liquor. They also found diminutive bars of soap, a modest sized first aid kit and a sewing kit.

Diana put all of the food items, which included six chocolate bars into a small cloth sack and handed it to Casey. "That's our food. You carry it. The chocolate bars should last us twelve days, if we each eat a quarter per day."

"That's not much food, is it?" She took the sack and tied it to a belt she had buckled around her coat.

"No, but there are other things like pine needles, berries and even some tree bark that is edible." Diana fashioned a shoelace sling for the small hand-axe and gave the piece of equipment to Casey. "You'll carry this one and I'll handle the big axe."

They strapped the metal pot and cups, and makeshift packs of blankets and other clothing to their backs and around their waists. Diana started laughing.

"What's so funny?"

"We must look like some kind of bums from the 1930's. I can just see us in a black and white movie, clunking and banging through the snow."

The vision made Casey laugh and she jumped wildly so that the cups clattered.

"Shh." Diana put her forefinger to her lips to silence Casey's giggling.

Casey look puzzled.

Diana pointed to some broken trees near the plane. "Look."

Casey looked in the direction and saw five or six dog-like creatures sniffing and prowling around the craft. "What are they?"

"Wolves. They are very curious creatures. That's what has been howling."

Casey whispered. "Will they hurt us?"

"No. But they'll get inside."

Even as she said it, two of the larger wolves jumped into the plane and disappeared. Several others pawed at debris on the ground and rooted into the lumps of snow that covered scattered baggage, as well as scattered bodies and body parts.

Casey seemed transfixed by the sight.

Diana spoke. "Come on, let's go. We've done all we could." She moved away from the shelter and began walking toward the hill that lay southwest of the craft. Casey trudged behind her. The cups tinkled softly.

The walking was easy across the open spot below the hill because all morning both Diana and Casey had walked back and forth in that area carrying pine boughs to fashion an arrow. The snow had been flattened by their constant footsteps. As they walked by the arrow, Diana commented. "It sure shows up in the snow, but if nobody sees it until spring, it won't do much good. It'll blend right in."

"You don't think we'll be here that long do you?"

"You never know what will happen. We could be found tomorrow or we could find help next week. All we can do is try."

The going up the hill was harder and it winded both of them. They stopped when they reached the top and turned to look back down to the small valley. The plane was almost completely hidden in the broken pines and the blanket of snow which covered it. The arrow, which had seemed so big when they were making it, looked small from this distance. Two of the wolves, one larger than the other, had left the others, who still prowled around the plane, and had followed the scent of Diana and Casey. They stopped at the foot of the hill and stared up at the two women, who were staring back at them.

"Are you sure they won't eat us?"

"Well, they do prefer warm meat as opposed to frozen varieties, but I wouldn't worry." Diana moved away from the hill and walked into the woods.

Casey jumped into action and glanced back over her shoulder. "That's not real reassuring." She was determined not to let Diana get too far ahead of her. The metal cups clattered as she forged ahead.

CHAPTER 14

During the latter part of the afternoon, the snowfall subsided and the wind stopped. The silence was overwhelming to Casey. She was not used to hearing nothing but the sound of her own breathing and the crunching of her own footfall in snow. The mist from her exhaled breath had formed a thin layer of ice on the scarf which covered her chin. When she drew air, the tips of her nostrils stung. She had never been this in touch with herself and with the environment. It seemed foreign to her and yet, she knew that what she was experiencing was a way of life for some people. She studied Diana as she moved ahead of her and wondered how it was that none of this seemed to bother her at all. Casey could not imagine that she, herself, would ever feel as at home in this place as Diana did.

The silence of the afternoon had an ethereal effect on Diana as she moved forward through the woods. She paused momentarily every once in a while to chop a quick notch in a tree. Someone would know what it meant, she was sure of that. She remembered that her father had told her that this area had once been the proud domain of the Chippewa tribe and that many of them lived in and around the Northern part of Wisconsin. They would know. She loved how the forest looked, so pristine and untouched by the onslaught of man and his civilization with its condos, high rises, malls, parking lots and miles and miles of concrete. This was clean, almost virgin. Diana knew that there were few places left where a person could get lost. Just be. Live off the land. She sighed as much from the burden of struggling through the snow as in remembering the mislaid dreams of youth.

The sigh broke her introspection and she thought about the woman who walked behind her. Casey seemed to her to be a person born into the middle of civilization, accustomed to malls and fast food and with no thought about her own mortality. Diana liked the woman, maybe too much, but they seemed to be worlds apart. She wondered if they would ever come to understand the world of the other. Probably not. There was not enough time for that unless one decided to commit to another. Diana had learned hard lessons about commitment and lost love. She sighed again. Stopped and notched a tree. Survival was all that mattered now.

Out of the corner of her eye, Diana caught a glimpse of some sort of rapid movement and she turned to her right, hoping to see clearly what had moved that quickly. She saw one and then another and then several more wolves. They were chasing a rabbit and in the deep snow, the unwary rabbit had strayed too far from its warren. It was no match for the lead wolf. In a few leaps the smaller wolf had captured the rabbit and with a quick snap, broke its neck. The group quickly tried to tear at the dead rabbit, but the largest wolf, an alpha, growled and the other wolves laid the dead rabbit down at the alpha's feet. The male wolf snatched the rabbit and tore at its skin and fur. Diana watched as the blood quickly stained the pure white snow. Casey had moved beside her and Diana could sense the fear in Casey.

"Don't worry. They only want the rabbit. They have been following us, but they're just curious. I think there are two pairs and they may be searching for territory of their own. The big one is the alpha. It's the dominate one and it happens to be a male and probably the oldest of the pack. All the others cater to the alpha. Actually, to the alpha pair." She stood looking at them, studying their movements.

"This is so foreign to me. I can't help it. It petrifies me."

"Don't panic. Wolves have been given a bad rap by ignorant people and those who stand to gain from their demise. They won't hurt us. After awhile they'll find where they want to be and we'll be long gone."

"Where they want to be?"

"Yeh. They're just looking for a home. Come on. We still have a few hours of daylight left." Diana move ahead again.

Casey took another look at the wolves. The smaller one was now eating parts of the snowshoe rabbit. The alpha wolf looked up at Casey. She thought he was beautiful, with his grey full coat and direct piercing eyes, but she was terrified and moved quickly to keep pace with Diana. She would not lag behind, if she could help it. She glanced back once more, but could no longer see the wolves. They had disappeared.

Only a bloody stain and a few tuffs of shredded fur remained in the snow.

CHAPTER 15

They had been walking and trudging and plunging through snow all afternoon. Their movements were rhythmic, automatic, tedious, labored; but always, they moved ahead.

Diana seemed driven by some unseen force to get somewhere, somewhere safe. Somewhere warm, secure, but the place was not there or just ahead. Ahead lay only more snow, more cedar and pine trees and brush and desolation. She would not let herself think of not finding safety. That was unthinkable. Safety in the form of shelter and food could be ever so near and she was determined to find it. When she thought about it, it was not so much for herself, but for the woman who trailed behind and for those who could not now or ever again find warmth or shelter or be with loved ones. She tried not to think of Sam or Randy, but she did and she thought of the little girl and the old man too. And, she thought of Urbano. Where could he be? She plunged ahead.

Casey was tired. Her legs seemed to be getting heavier and heavier. Her knees were stiff and yet at the same time, rubbery. She felt like she would just collapse. The thought was not bad. Collapsing would give her a chance to rest. She could not keep up with Diana, and although the fear of the wolves had made her adrenaline flow and gave her added energy and strength, the strenuous walking through the snow had taken its toll. She was lagging further and further behind Diana. She just could not go any more. Casey stopped and leaned on a tree trunk. The wind had picked up in velocity and was blowing the icy snow around in little swirls. She bowed her head to keep her bare face out of the wind and that is when she saw a hand sticking out of the snow just to the left of the tree she leaned upon.

She screamed. "Oh, my God. Diana. Diana."

Diana stopped her forward motion and turned back to look at Casey. She could not see what caused Casey's fright because blowing snow obscured her vision. She ran toward the woman, yelling, "What is it? What's the matter?"

Casey pointed down to the snow.

Diana got to her and looked down. A hand, frozen, and clinched into a fist was sticking out of a drift. A rosary dangled from the stiff fingers and swayed in the gusts of wind.

"Oh, no. It must be Urbano." She knelt down and pushed snow away. Within several minutes of effort, she had uncovered Urbano's face. He appeared to be sleeping. His eyelashes were silvery white with snow and frost. The skin was ashen. His face looked like some sort of mask, unreal. He looked like all the others who were left in the plane. A person frozen in time.

Casey looked at Urbano and felt a twinge of sorrow. "He was afraid out here, you know?"

"I know." Diana stood up and began digging into her pockets.

"Is it painful? The dying?"

"No. He just went to sleep. We need to cover him up again, but first, I want to leave something with him." Diana pulled her hand out of her pocket. In her hand, she held the knife she had taken from him at the airport. She looked at it a moment and then bent down and put it into his jacket pocket.

Casey asked, "Why'd you do that?"

"I promised him he would get it back, but I wish it didn't have to be like this." She began to push snow back over Urbano's face and upper body. In a few minutes the task was done. She took the double-bit axe and chopped a cross in the tree which Casey had been leaning upon.

"Can't we stop, Diana? I'm cold and hungry."

"Not here. Not now." Diana looked at her watch. We still have another hour of day light.

Casey began to shiver. "Maybe we should go back to the wreck."

"I won't stay there. Not with those bodies. Not with hunger." Diana started to move away from the site.

"You would eat them, wouldn't you?"

"Maybe I would. So what?"

"Good God, Diana. We're civilized. I thought that the primary reason we left the site was that no one was looking for us."

"Maybe you're right about no one looking for us, but you're wrong about not eating them. Civilized has nothing to do with extreme hunger."

Casey became indignant. "In my book it does."

Diana swung the axe at a tree and it stuck, hanging like a wedge. She glared at Casey. "Out here, your book doesn't count. Survival counts. And anyway you can get it, you'll get it."

"Not everyone feels that way."

"Oh, yeh? You think Urbano wouldn't have done anything to survive? Shit. He would have taken the first bite and I would have been right behind him."

"Well, I'm not Urbano and I'm no animal either."

Diana reached out and jerked the axe from the tree. "Animal? Yes, I guess you're right. You haven't reached the point where your instinct takes over and keeps you from killing yourself."

"What's that suppose to mean?"

Diana stared straight into Casey's eyes as she spoke. "Urbano was an animal. A street animal. Too bad he was ignorant about the other animal in himself. That's the one thing that could have saved him." She looked down at the snow-covered figure and then back at Casey. "I'm going on. With or without you." She turned from Casey and walked further into the woods.

Casey hesitated only a moment and then she reluctantly followed in the footsteps that Diana had left in the snow. She was cold and scared, but she knew that her only hope lay in staying with the woman who was so unbending. She had never met anyone like Diana or if she had, she did not know it. She struggled in her mind to understand the single-mindedness and seeming inflexibility of the woman who now trudged doggedly ahead of her through the woods in search of security for them both. She was not sure that she would ever understand her or for that matter, that it mattered if she did or not. She only knew that she was drawn toward Diana in a way she found disturbing. If she did not know better, Casey would have to admit that she was interested in knowing everything she could about Diana. And that sort of curiosity about someone was usually reserved for someone who was romantically intriguing. The thought stopped her. She stared blankly at the woman who pushed through the snow ahead of her.

Diana turned back to look for Casey and seeing her stopped, she yelled back. "Come on. We have to keep moving for another hour before we can stop. Come on."

Casey followed. There would be no turning back now. The journey had begun for real.

CHAPTER 16

Diana continued notching trees as she moved through the forest. Occasionally she turned to look back at Casey. They had not spoken to one another for over half an hour. Snow had begun to fall once again and the chill of the cold air cut through Diana's jacket. She knew that Casey must be very cold, but she would not think about stopping for at least another hour. She had not found anything yet that indicated that other people were nearby or that any sort of help was readily available. She had hoped to find a stream by now, but none was in sight, so she trudged forward.

Behind her, Casey had long ago felt the sting of the cold. She had wanted to stop but she no longer tried to make a case, for she knew that Diana was determined to walk until some self appointed time elapsed. Whatever the plan was, only Diana seemed to know it. Casey simply followed. As she struggled to keep pace, she thought of food. The cold had made her hungry, so she reached inside the small bag and pulled out a candy bar. She pulled at the wrapper with her teeth. It split open and the smell of chocolate assaulted her nostrils. For a moment, she smiled and then, she ate the whole bar. It tasted good. Smudges of chocolate stuck to her gloves and she licked at them hungrily. Up ahead, Diana moved down a steep slope and stopped at the bottom. Casey leaned against a tree at the top of the incline and finished licking her lips and savoring the chocolate surge that raced through her being.

Diana bent down and brushed at the snow on the ground. She stood up and swung the double bit high above her head and brought it hard upon the ground. There was a cracking sound and suddenly water gushed through a hole. Diana was instantly excited. "By God, now we're in luck. I've found a stream."

Casey yelled down to her. "What does that mean?"

"It means that we will eventually find other people."

Casey slipped and slid down the incline to where Diana stood. "I don't understand. How? When?"

"Look, this is a good place to stop." Diana was excited. "I should take time to make snowshoes, but…" She looked at Casey and realized she hadn't answered anything. "Tomorrow we'll follow the stream that way." She pointed down stream.

"But, why? And, what about people?"

"The stream flows that way. Sooner or later, it will come to a bigger stream and maybe an even bigger one. That's when we'll find people. Out here, water is very important. But more important, is being near it. So we'll find someone who lives near a stream." Diana threw off her pack and began cutting small boughs off nearby fir trees.

Casey stared at the water. It all seemed so simple when Diana said it, but she was not so sure about it. The whack of the axe on the tree limbs broke her thoughts. She took off her pack, laid it on the snow near a pine tree, bent down and began clearing the snow off the ground.

Diana threw half a dozen boughs in her direction. "Take some of the larger ones and jam them into the snow at an angle. Prop them up anyway you can. I'll go try to find some dry wood for a fire."

Casey just nodded at her. She retrieved the cut limbs and began to jam them into the higher snow near the base of the incline. In a short time, she had fashioned a small lean-to. She began again to push snow away from the shelter. When her efforts resulted in clearing away most of the snow down to the ground, she took some of the smaller pine boughs and spread them on the ground inside the shelter. She was tired, but she felt a sense of accomplishment.

Diana returned with an armload of sticks and small pieces of broken pin oak limbs, the dead leaves still clinging to them. She dropped them on the ground near the shelter. She studied the lean-to. "Good job, Casey. You might become self sufficient, if you aren't careful."

Casey smiled. At last, a compliment.

"I'll cut some more limbs after I get our fire started."

Diana grabbed her pack and undid it. She pulled a piece of newspaper out and ripped off a sheet and crumpled it. Then she placed it down on the ground and carefully stacked small twigs on top of the crumpled paper.

"This is cheating, but I don't care." She smiled up at Casey as she struck a match. She looked down and watched the flame ignite the paper and speed on to combust the twigs. She added larger pieces of wood and the fire ate them.

Casey stooped down to warm her hands over the flames. They crouched on opposite sides of the small fire and let the warmth take the sting out of the cold that permeated them both. Diana smiled at Casey and Casey smiled back.

Diana spoke. "I'll finish the shelter. Take the pot and get some water. We have the whole night to keep warm and to drink pine needle broth."

Casey put her hands on her face and let them warm her cheeks. She crouched that way for a moment, then retrieved the battered metal pot from her pack and headed toward the hole Diana had chopped in the ice. When she returned with the water, she found that Diana had already fashioned a makeshift teabag out of a handkerchief and some pine needles. She sat down on a blanket inside the shelter next to Diana and handed her the pot.

"You are about to experience living off the land." She smiled as she reached for the food pouch that Casey had been carrying." We'll have a chocolate wedge to go with the brew." She emptied the contents out onto the blanket. She frowned. "There are only five candy bars here."

Casey looked at her. "I ate one."

Diana's voice raised an octave. "A whole one?"

Casey was instantly defensive. "Yes, dammit. I'm hungry."

"You're going to be a hell of a lot hungrier before this is over. I'm splitting the food. I'll keep my own share."

Casey was stung. "One candy bar. Big deal."

"Don't you understand? I don't know where we are, or when we'll find people and food and shelter. This is all we have." Diana put her share into her jacket pocket.

"We could find civilization tomorrow."

"And maybe a month from now. You just ate four days in one day." Diana threw a larger log on the fire.

"So what?"

The arrogance in the comment angered Diana. She turned to stare straight into Casey's violet eyes. "So I'll tell you what. If you want to eat your entire share right now, do it. But don't try to get mine. I'll kill you if you try."

Casey was stung. She turned away and stared out into the forest. A mixture of fear and anger burned inside her.

Diana retrieved the steaming pot of water from near the fire and made two cups of pine needle broth. She nudged Casey's arm and gave her a cup. She did not speak to her. She reached inside her coat and pulled out a candy bar and proceeded to eat a very small portion of it and then replaced it in her pocket. The fire crackled. She stole a sidelong glance at Casey, who nursed her drink. Diana liked the woman, but she feared that she was too civilized and Diana knew that that flaw might kill them both. She turned back to the fire and stared into the dancing flames while she finished her drink. She set her cup far back in the shelter and wrapped herself with a blanket. She lay down and promptly drifted off to sleep.

Casey sat staring into the fire. Snow drifted inside the lean-to and settled on her eyelashes. She looked out into the dark, afraid of the shadows and the unknown. She only knew about ad campaigns, creating slogans and selling people via television. Nothing in her life had prepared her for this. Absolute fear gripped her whole being. She did not want to die, unloved and uncelebrated in some godforsaken place. She whispered, "There has to be a way out. There just has to be."

Casey pulled a blanket close and wrapped it around her body. She moved further inside the shelter and lay awake, her mind not able to shut down as her fears stabbed at her heart.

In the distance, a mournful wailing howl echoed through the woods, reverberating off the stately pine trees, and resounding across eons to time to be captured by the ears of a woman who did not understand what she heard.

Next to her, Diana slept in peace.

CHAPTER 17

It was snowing lightly as the single engine Cessna 152 taxied up to the tie-down area near the Hayward airport terminal. Martin Forrester shut down the engine and emerged from the small plane. He tied a line to the left wing and the tail section, making sure they were secure. Joe Finney exited the craft from the right side and secured the right wing. They walked to the small terminal.

Al Hartman looked up from the table in the center of the room as they entered. "Hi. How'd it go?"

Finney answered. "We got clear over to Black Lake, then north to Little Moose River. Nothing." He sat down at the table and lit a cigarette. "We criss-crossed all the way back to Chippewa River and south down to the area around Moose Lake. Not a damn sign of anything. Hell, I'm half blind squintin' in this snow."

Martin poured himself a cup of coffee and one for Joe. He set Joe's cup on the table and walked over to the wall chart.

Joe said, "Mark off that section. Jesus, two weeks and we ain't seen nothin' but snow."

Martin crossed off the section with a black felt-tip pen and stood studying the map. "I had no idea that Wisconsin was this desolate. When Cramer and the others in Chicago said there wasn't much up here, I never dreamed it would look like this."

Al chuckled. "You have to understand, that area over there is in the Chequamegon National Forest. We're talkin' real primitive. It's sort of like what trappers encountered when they first came here. A lot of lakes, a lot of beavers, a lot of scenery."

Joe added, "Yeh, trees, animals and real sparse on people."

Martin walked to the table and sat down. "Where do you think we should look next?"

Joe stubbed out his cigarette. "Ah…well…Look Martin, when the search group stopped looking last week…it…I mean…they…"

"What are you trying to say?"

Joe looked to Al for support.

Martin caught the look. "Out with it. What is it?"

Joe sucked in air. "Nobody wants to give up, but…there comes a time when you know…in weather like this…I mean the cold being what it is……"

Al took up the slack. "What he's trying to say is nobody figures that anyone could survive in this weather for almost two weeks without food or a warm shelter. People just can't do it anymore."

"You don't know my girl."

Joe continued. "We don't doubt what you say, but be realistic. The group flew hundreds of square miles without seeing the downed plane."

Al shuffled weather reports. "Weather service is predicting another Artic front to move in and this one is supposed to be producing an even heavier snowfall than the first one. If we could locate the craft, maybe we'd feel differently about abandoning the search."

"Dammit, guys, that's the point. If we locate the craft, then we should know right away if anyone survived." Martin's eyes pleaded with them.

Joe shook his head. "Wherever it is, it's buried good. And every time it snows, it gets covered even more. We could've flown right over it and just not seen it. We can't keep flying back over hundreds of miles."

Martin pushed away from the table in frustration. "I can't give up." He stood up and faced them defiantly. "Don't you see that? My girl, my flesh and blood is out there somewhere. I can't quit."

Al's face reddened. "We want to help, but there's only so much we can do. We're not your enemy, Forrester. Your enemy is out there and we can't change it and we can't fight it. We have to just live with it."

Martin moved to the front window and stared out at the snow, sensing the cold and knowing the odds against his wish, his hope.

"And maybe Diana can live with it too." He turned to them and spoke matter-of-factly. "I won't give up. Every chance I get, I'm going to look. You can count on that."

Joe and Al exchanged looks, but neither knew how to respond.

Al stared at the papers before him and saw a memo. "Oh, almost forgot. A guy by the name of Frank Rawlins called here for you."

Martin looked puzzled. "Frank Rawlins? I don't know anybody by…huh…the name does sound familiar. Oh, yeh, the woman at Drake Airlines mentioned his name."

"He didn't say what he wanted. He just left a number and said to call him when you had time." Al extended the memo toward Martin. "It appears to be a Chicago number. Might be something about the craft."

Martin looked at the number. "Thanks. I do appreciate you hanging in there after the official search was called off. I know you have other things to do."

Joe blew smoke from a cigarette he had just lit. "Hey, don't go apologizing. We want to help. It's just that time forces us to go on with our lives. I'll gladly help you on my days off. You know that."

Al added. "I'll be here as usual. Keeping the coffee hot. Every time a local goes up, he'll look. Sooner or later, one of 'em will spot it."

Martin walked over to the chart which had so many areas crossed off that it looked like a checkered flag. He ran his right hand over the map. "It's a vast wild area. A lot of people probably have been lost out there."

Joe said. "Yeh. No doubt."

Martin continued. "Diana has a pioneer spirit. I guess that's why I can't give up. Even if she didn't survive the crash, she'd expect me to search for her, because she grew up knowing that I'd expect her to look for me if I was lost. Dead or alive, it's all the same. You have to find your family when they're lost and bring them home."

Joe and Al said nothing.

Martin put his wool knit cap on and zippered his parka. He moved to the back door. "You'll see me again. When the weather breaks some, I'll be back."

He saluted them and left.

Al got up from the table and walked to the coffee pot in the pilot room. He poured himself a cup and stirred the sugar slowly as he walked back to the main room.

Joe spoke. "You know what?"

"What?"

"There's something about him that makes me believe he will find his daughter alive. I know that sounds crazy, what with the weather and the circumstances, but…"

Al cut in, "Naw, it doesn't sound crazy to me. I can't quite put my finger on it. I guess I'd just say it was faith or something like that." He drank some coffee.

Joe leaned back in his chair and blew a smoke ring. "Yeh. Or maybe a father's love for his child."

CHAPTER 18

❦

Snow devils whirled wildly through the pine and pin oak as the two bent figures struggled to wade through the snow near the edge of the frozen stream. The makeshift snowshoes that Diana had made for them ten days before slapped at the snow. Most of the slender wood webbing was broken and the snowshoes soon would be useless. They plodded forward. On top of the ridge above them, two wolves watched and when the figures moved ahead, they moved ahead. When they stopped, the wolves stopped.

Diana led the way, but she was tired and hungry and although she would not admit it to Casey, physically and even mentally weak. The elements were taking their toll. She seldom notched trees anymore, for the effort took too much out of her. Casey never asked about it and for that she was thankful. The woman had surprised her by staying alive and by keeping up with her, but now, Diana knew unless something dramatic happened, they were doomed. The thought angered her.

She stopped and used her teeth to pull off a mitten and a sock that covered her right hand, and then pulled off the left mitten and sock. Mechanically, she reached into her coat pocket and extracted a crumpled candy wrapper. Her fingers struggled in the cold to remove the small piece of chocolate. She put it in her mouth and just let the tiny lump lay there while she sucked every bit of nourishment she could from it. She reached inside her pocket again, but there were only small scraps and bits of empty paper. The pieces blew away in the wind. She watched after them until they were gone in a swirl of snow.

Casey came up behind her and placed her hand on Diana's shoulder. She said in a weak voice, "I can't go much further. Not today, please."

Diana could not bear to look at Casey, for she wore a mask that portrayed death. Grey and listless. She spoke, not turning around. "Okay. We'll stop here."

Casey dropped her pack in the snow. She moved toward some fallen branches in an effort to secure some firewood.

Diana simply let her pack fall and lie where it fell. She moved slowly toward some pine trees that grew along the diminishing incline to her right. The double-bit axe felt as though it weighed fifty pounds. She could not give a full swing with it, only small strokes, but even still, it cut the pine boughs off the trees with little effort. The bit edges were sharp. The chopped boughs fell in ever increasing number. Behind her, Casey hacked at cedar boughs with the small hand axe.

They each knew their jobs now and the movements and efforts were mechanical, robot-like. No need to think, just do. Survival was no longer talked about. They simply did what they had to do from day to day. Walk, make a shelter. Walk, make a shelter.

Casey dragged some of her cut boughs to where the packs lay. She kicked off her shabby snowshoes and began to fashion a shelter. It was haphazard, but it would have to do. She stuck the branches into the snow and tried to form a roof, a wind block, a snow block. She could not remember what day it was, but then it occurred to her that it really did not matter what day it was. It was all the same. As she worked, Casey heard the chop of Diana's axe ringing in her ears. Then it was silent. She thought she heard voices. She stopped and looked toward Diana.

Diana had fallen in the snow and lay there, not moving.

Casey yelled, "Diana!"

No response.

With effort, Casey went to where Diana lay. She shook her.

"Are you okay?"

Diana's eyes fluttered opened. "Yeh. Just tired." She sat up. "I'll be okay."

Casey was somewhat excited, "We must be near a town. I think I heard voices somewhere. And I'm positive I smelled coffee. Did you hear the voices?"

Diana struggled to stand. Her snowshoes were broken. She kicked them aside. She reached out and enveloped Casey in her arms and stroked her back. She fought back tears. "I didn't hear anything but the wind, Casey. Help me get this wood back to the shelter. I'll make a fire. We'll have some pine broth. That'll taste good."

Casey searched Diana's eyes for some kind of assurance. She bit her lip. "I could have sworn I heard people...and the coffee...it was so real."

Diana said nothing. She dragged pieces of fallen branches and pine boughs back to the shelter. It was not much of a shelter, but it would have to do.

Casey managed to pick up some wood and came behind her. She let the wood fall and knelt down to push snow away from the helter-skelter lean-to. Diana helped. They did not bother to make a big place for themselves, for it took too much effort.

Diana sat down in the small snow cleared area in front of the shelter. "Hand me your hand axe."

Casey gave it to her.

The snow stopped, not altogether, for there were small flakes that drifted here and there, but it had stopped. A shaft of evening sunlight streaked through the forest. They stopped their efforts to make a fire and looked in stunned disbelief as the light seemingly danced across the tops of pine, bare oak and maple trees. A ray of sun hit an open patch of water in the frozen stream and a blaze of light washed across their faces. Large cumulus clouds broke apart and the blue of a winter sky transfixed their gaze.

They sat for some time in silence, looking at something that they had not seen for over two weeks. Sunlight. Pure sunlight. It was beautiful. As the sun dropped near the horizon, the clouds turned pink, orange, and finally, flame red. The sun set and a dusky grey evening began.

Diana used the hand axe to cut slivers of wood from some of the larger pieces of timber they had gathered. Casey broke twigs into small pieces and stacked them at Diana's feet. Diana extracted a match from her backpack and with shaking hands, lit the fire. The twigs snapped and crackled.

Casey put a larger piece of wood on top of the twigs and watched as the flames licked at the bark. She stared at it, unaware that Diana had inched back into the shelter and had fallen asleep.

Casey spoke. "I know I heard people. It sounded like a lot of people. Didn't you hear them?"

No response.

Casey turned and saw that Diana slept. She watched the slow breathing of one in deep sleep and she did not want to wake her.

She pulled the beat-up metal pot from her backpack and set about the task of making pine needle broth. It no longer tasted like *Pine Sol* to her. She had grown to like it, for it was food and now it was the only food they had. Patterns in her life were changing as the days passed. Casey no longer thought about million dollar clients, for they did not matter. She could not even remember the name of the client who waited in Duluth.

The snow melted in the pot. Casey added a pine needle pouch and watched the greenish yellow color seep into the water. The smell of *Pine Sol* assaulted her nose. She managed to smile. On impulse, she leaned over and kissed Diana's cheek. There was no response.

Casey turned back to the fire and watched it glow red and yellow against the darkening sky.

Above her, a full moon danced among the stars.

CHAPTER 19

Billowing cumulus clouds moved across the star filled night and, in the cold air, the moon cast brilliant light through the forest. The night was bright, so bright that it seemed to be day. Creatures moved easily and silently through the woods in search of food and prey.

Smoke floated skyward from the orange and yellow embers of the dying fire at the campsite Diana and Casey had made. Inside the shelter, both Diana and Casey slept. Casey's left arm was wrapped around Diana and in her right hand, she clutched her hand axe. Except for occasional crackling from the fire, the night was silent, still, and mystical in the moonlight.

Across the small creek, a pair of wolves stood staring at the camp. Their eyes glowed. A cloud passed overhead and briefly covered the moon. The larger wolf tilted his head back and howled. The howl pierced the night with a sudden wail that startled all the nearby creatures.

And, the sound interrupted the nightmare that plagued Casey's sleep. She sat up with a start. Frightened, disoriented. The moonlight blazed across the snow. She jumped to her feet, flailing the hand axe. She let out a monstrous scream. Then she started running up the slight incline, screaming as she went.

The murderous commotion awoke Diana. Adrenalin rushed through her body. She jumped to her feet and looked toward the direction in which Casey had run. She could clearly see Casey stumbling, half running in the deep snow up the incline. Moonlight glinted off the hand axe. Diana saw the axe and was spurred into action. She ran after Casey, sensing that the woman was delirious and she feared that Casey would hurt herself.

The wolves watched the scene in silence.

Casey stumbled and struck out with the hand axe at the small pine trees that blocked her flight. It was as though someone or something was chasing her and she would not let the demon catch her. She ran as best she could in the snow, but the action seemed as though it was done in slow motion. The snow grabbed at her feet. She could hear the thing behind her yelling her name, but she knew it was a trick and she would not stop. Safety would come. It had too. Ahead of her, the moonlight silhouetted what appeared to be a large doorway, an arch. That would be her safety. The demon was getting closer. She heard the labored breathing behind her.

When Diana got to the top of the incline, she could not see Casey, for small pine trees blocked her view, but she could see the path through the snow where Casey had run. Diana yelled for her, but there was no answer. She crashed through the small trees and came out on the other side. A small cabin and a log arched deer rack stood bathed in moonlight. The sight overwhelmed Diana. She screamed Casey's name, but Casey did not stop. The woman seemed to be pursued by some imaginary devils. Diana ran after her. The exercise was too much, she puffed and blew, inhaled, exhaled. Her breathing was loud and labored. She was within close proximity of Casey, who had just reached the deer dressing rack.

Casey spun around and raised the hand axe over her head. "You can't get me now. I am safe. This is my safety." She swung the axe over her head with both gloved hands.

Diana realized that Casey was in the throes of a hallucination. When she saw the axe raised above Casey's head, she was convinced that Casey was delirious and dangerous. She threw herself sideways just as the flash of the blade came downward. Diana fell into the snow. She expected to feel the blow, but nothing hit her. She rolled sideways and struggled to her feet.

Casey lay crumpled face down in the snow. Quiet and unmoving.

Diana moved cautiously toward her. The moon danced from behind a cloud and the light revealed a dark stain in the snow near Casey's right leg. Diana knew instantly what she saw and fear gripped her whole being. She knelt down and carefully rolled Casey on her back. The hand-axe, which lay beneath Casey, was covered with blood. Diana pushed it aside. Moonlight revealed the large tear in Casey's right pant leg. She pulled the trouser material apart to locate the wound, and blood oozed from a gaping slash in Casey's upper thigh. Diana bit her lip.

She calmed herself by saying out loud the time old words. "This calls for directed activity. Directed activity." She pulled her scarf from around her neck and tied it just above the slash. She looked around for a branch and quickly located some stacked kindling next to one of the trees that helped form the deer rack. Diana grabbed a small piece of wood and used it to tighten the makeshift tourniquet. The blood flow began to subside. She lightly rubbed snow on Casey's face.

Casey's eyes opened. A wild look momentarily covered her face.

Diana pressed her body against Casey and whispered into her ear. "You've been hurt Casey, but it will be all right. I will help you." She kissed her cheek. "I need you to help me now."

"My legs hurt. I'm so tired." She sighed.

Diana knew that whatever delirium had consumed Casey within the last five minutes was gone and that Casey was back to reality. Diana sat up and looked directly into Casey's face. "We have to get to the cabin that is just over there." She pointed.

Casey struggled to sit. "A cabin?" She looked toward the small log cabin that was nestled among towering white pine and spruce trees surrounded with a canopy of stately oak and maple limbs and branches. She said again in disbelief of what her eyes told her, "A cabin?"

"Yes, a cabin." Diana twisted the tourniquet.

Casey looked down at her leg and gasped. "Oh, God." She swooned.

"Don't faint, not now. God, Casey. I can't carry you there. I'm too weak from hunger. Please, don't faint."

Casey sucked in air.

"It'll be okay. You have to walk as best as you can. Lean on me. Help me get you there. It's our only hope now."

Casey sucked in more air. "I can do it. I'll help." Tears of pain and fear streaked her face as she struggled to her feet.

"You hang on to the stick and keep it tight." Diana steadied Casey as she moved to the left side of her and put her right arm around her waist. She pulled Casey's left arm up over her shoulder and grasped her wrist with her left hand. In that fashion, they walked and staggered to the cabin.

The building had long been abandoned. Several of the rough sawn boards that made up the floor of the porch were broken and they had to carefully make their way to the entrance. The door was sturdy, but unlocked. When they entered, the smell of years of dust and mildew assaulted their noses, but neither seemed to mind, for the building represented salvation to them. The pine floor creaked and groaned under their footsteps. Shafts of moonlight entered the room through a window on the south side of the cabin. The window on the other side and two in the front also emitted light. Diana was delighted to see that a huge field stone fireplace dominated the back wall of the structure. To the right of the single room cabin was a makeshift bed, big enough for two people, but not much on comfort, for its bed was simply made of thick planks of sawed wood. For now, it would do.

Diana eased Casey down upon the wooden planks. And almost immediately, Casey went limp. As Diana pushed back the lids on Casey's eyes, a shaft of moonlight filtered through the window that was above the bed and she could see that Casey's eyes were rolled back. The woman had passed out. She was thankful for that. She pushed her toward the wall and retightened the tourniquet.

Diana gave the cabin a cursory look and noticed a wooden table and three wooden chairs to the left side. There was a counter along the left wall and above it were two wooden cabinets. She wanted to explore its possibilities, but there was no time for that now. She knew that she had to retrieve their packs and find something with which to close the wound on Casey's leg. She could not remember what they had brought from the plane. The crash had happened so long ago that time seemed endless.

She took one last look at Casey and felt a flood of emotion well within her. To have come so far and to be so close to surviving. It was unthinkable that she might lose her only companion. She would not allow that to happen. The weakness that had overcome her body these past few days was abated by the fear that gripped her. Somewhere within her, the strength to carry-on surfaced and Diana ran from the cabin toward the packs that lay just down the slight incline near the creek.

As Diana ran, she realized that her fear was based on something more than just the potential loss of a companion. Diana had to admit to herself that she had fallen in love with the woman who lay injured and possibly near death. This was not Casey's world, but Casey was becoming less and less dependent and more and more self-sufficient. Whatever Casey's weaknesses were, Diana had seen her strengths and that is what had made her love for Casey grow. She could not die, not now. Not now. Diana was determined to do everything she could to keep her alive.

When she came to the lean-to, the two wolves were sniffing around the site. Startled, they looked up as she approached, and the larger of the two leaped toward her. Diana fell backwards expecting to be attacked, but the wolf bounded past her and the other followed, never even looking back.

"Well, I'll be damned. Maybe I've found others to love." She called after them. "You can be my wild love." She turned to the shelter and saw Casey's backpack and added, "And the other love, I'll keep hidden and to myself until the time is right."

CHAPTER 20

Diana walked through the cluster of young white pine, dragging the packs with her left hand and carrying the double-bit axe in her right hand. Light from the moon made the night seem as though it was just an overcast day. In the brightness, as she emerged from the pines, she saw a wolf near the deer rack where Casey had hurt herself. The wolf was pawing in the snow, sniffing and emitting whining sounds. Its mate, which stood by a tree near the rack, waiting and watching, spotted Diana and ran to nudge the other wolf. Their yellow eyes glowed at her.

Diana raised the axe in defiance and the smaller wolf ran a short distance away. The larger wolf looked at her, then turned and slowly walked to its waiting mate. The two loped away into the forest. Diana was glad that she did not have to challenge them for territory, because what little strength she had left, had to be used to build a fire and do something about the gash in Casey's leg. She approached the spot where the wolves had been and saw again the large bloodstain that marked the snow. The hand-axe lay in the pool of blood. She retrieved it and went to the cabin.

Moonlight streamed in through the window near the bed and in the light, Diana could make out more of the features inside the cabin. The most important thing she noticed was that someone, long ago had left wood near the fireplace and, although it was riddled with insect holes, it would serve the immediate purpose of providing the makings for a fire. She looked at Casey and noted that she was still out cold. The leg had stopped bleeding, but it needed to be closed up. But, first the fire.

In hardly any time at all, Diana had stacked small twigs on the stone floor of the fireplace. She lit a match and the dry twigs caught immediately. She carefully placed larger pieces of wood on the flames and watched as the pine and oak flared up into roaring, flaming heat. The light illuminated the room, as Diana placed the two packs on the wooden table and began rummaging through them.

The first aid kit had the usual pressure pads, gauze, tape, scissors and tweezers, but there was nothing with which to close the wound. Diana dug around again and produced an assortment of miniature liquor bottles of rum, whiskey and vodka.

"Damn, I forgot we had these." She looked at Casey. "Wonder if I could knock her out with this stuff?" She set the bottles aside and dug further into Casey's backpack. She pulled out a small plastic box which contained an assortment of needles and ten different packets of nylon thread. She smiled.

"Well, we're getting closer to operation time. Too bad I don't have some knock out drops or something, but I have the most important things."

She walked over to the fireplace in order to inspect the needles in the kit. In the firelight, Diana saw that her hands and nails were filthy from weeks of being unwashed and she was ashamed. She knew that she couldn't do what she had to do unless they were washed and for that matter, she knew she would have to wash the area around Casey's thigh. She remembered they had taken small bars of soap from the plane and that somewhere in her pack those bars were still wrapped and waiting to be used. She returned to her backpack, turned it upside down and more than a dozen small bars of soap bounced upon the table among an assortment of shoelaces, matchbooks and other odds and ends. She was closer now to really doing the job. The only thing left was to get some warm water.

The metal pot they had used for broth was not big enough. Against all hope, Diana began to look around the cabin and in the corner to the right of the front door, she spotted a metal bucket.

"Oh, my God." She grabbed it and ran outside. In the moonlight, she turned it over and over, inspecting it to see if there were any splits in its seams along the side or in the bottom. It was dented and beat up, but it was free of any holes.

She cleaned it with snow and then hurriedly packed it with clean snow, went back inside the cabin and hung it on the iron rod that swung over and above the fire in the fireplace.

She retrieved the needles from the sewing kit and extracted the longest one. She looked at it a moment and realized that somehow she would have to bend it. It was not easy, but Diana put the needle in the door hinge and with a little pressure, bent the needle into a vee shape. Before she could begin the job of sewing Casey's leg she would have to wash her hands and the leg.

Diana spoke out loud, "If she survives, she's going to have one hell of a scar." She looked at Casey, then moved to the steaming bucket of water and began to prepare for the job at hand.

Outside the cabin, the orange glow from the fireplace shone through the windows and beckoned to the pair of wolves who watched. It was quiet and then a yowling sound startled the wolves. Their ears stood up and they twisted their heads as though trying to interpret what they heard. The yowl came again and again. The male alpha wolf raised his head and howled an answer. He waited expectantly. Nothing.

The night was silent and no more sounds echoed through the woods. Fragrant smoke drifted through the forest while the moon danced among the heavens and a million stars twinkled in the clean clear cold air.

And so, the evening passed.

CHAPTER 21

Steam rose from the *Bunn* pot. The old reliable coffee maker whined as the steady stream of dark liquid filled the waiting glass container.

Joe stood by the front window of the shack, smoking and staring outside. He turned at the sound. "Well, it's singing. It must be done. Anybody, besides me, want some?"

Al looked up from his desk. "Sure, light on the cream."

He swiveled in his chair to look at the calendar, and then reached up with a felt tip to mark off the eighth of February.

Martin, seated at the round table, watched Al, but spoke to Joe. "I'll take black." Then he said to no one in particular. "Time does fly, doesn't it?"

As he passed by, Joe set a cup of coffee in front of Martin and handed Al his cup. He stepped back to the table and sat down.

"What time is this guy suppose to be here?"

"When I talked to him last week, he figured that he'd be in by mid morning, if the roads were decent. For once, luck's with us. So he should be rolling in anytime."

Joe asked, "What's the story?"

"According to this Rawlins, who was one of the mechanics for Drake, the craft had some problems prior to takeoff. Rawlins hadn't always worked on that plane, so he didn't know the total history. He claims he had a hell of a row with Drake about letting the plane go."

Al got up from the desk and moved to the table. "So why did he? Hell, he has to be a certified A and P mechanic."

"Yeh, he is. But he had a drinking problem, got fired from a job six months ago and damn near lost his license. That's when Drake picked him up. He says he has his liquor under control, but he was still afraid of losing his job."

Joe lit a cigarette. "What'd he tell the Feds?"

"Nothing. Drake let him know that if he said anything, he'd claim Rawlins was drunk on the job and that he'd see that he lost his license forever."

Al shook his head. "Drake sounds like a real son of a bitch."

"I'll reserve that thought until I talk to Rawlins. He might be trying to cover himself. The feds will rip those maintenance records apart." Martin sipped his coffee.

The front door to the shack opened with a bang as a short, heavyset man with curly blond hair and a ruddy face entered.

Martin stood up. "Are you Frank?"

"Yeh." He brushed snow off his quilted blue parka.

Martin walked to him and extended his hand. "I'm Martin Forrester. Glad you made it." He turned to the others. "Frank, this is Al Hartman, airport manager. And this is Joe Finney, Civil Air Patrol."

Rawlins walked over to the table and shook hands. "Damn cold out there, huh?"

Joe smiled, "Sure is. Want a cup of coffee?"

"Sounds good to me. Just a little sugar." He pulled off his coat and hung it on the back of a chair, then sat down at the table with Martin and Al.

Martin studied the man's face. "I filled them in on our phone conversation."

Joe set coffee in front of Frank and eased down in the remaining seat at the table. He leaned back in his chair and lit a cigarette.

Rawlins nodded a "thank you" to Joe and then said to Martin. "A lot's happened since I talked to you. For one thing, Drake doesn't know where I am. I told him I had to get away for a few days. He didn't object because the feds were starting to ask questions that Carl didn't want answered."

"Like what?"

"The FAA people weren't convinced that Jackson...he was the pilot that flew just before Sam...was telling them the truth about the condition of the plane. See, Jackson told me a vague story about a radio problem and a possible problem with the nav system. Drake told Jackson that he better think about protecting his job before he got `too careless', as he put it, with his story."

Al shook his head. "You mean this guy lied to the feds about the aircraft?"

Frank pulled a pack of cigarettes from his shirt pocket.

"He didn't exactly lie and that was the trouble. Jackson tried to be evasive, but hell, the guy is too honest. The feds knew he was covering something. He was too damn shaky." He tapped his cigarette on the table.

Joe took a swig of coffee. "God damn. This is a real mess."

"Go on," Martin said. "Tell me more." Anger burned at the back of his neck.

"Well, the Feds came to me and I told them to check the maintenance records. They said they had and that everything looked to be in order. I couldn't believe it."

"So what'd you do?" Joe asked as he snubbed out his cigarette. He folded his hands and leaned into the table, intent.

"First chance I got, I looked at the records on that crate. They were doctored. I can't vouch for anything back beyond six months ago, but I know there was some stuff missing. I worked on the nav system once myself. That wasn't even in there."

Martin slammed his fist down on the table, startling them all.

"What you're telling us then, is that Drake is hiding something that could be damaging to him."

"You got it. Hell, I didn't want the plane to fly that night because Jackson said he had problems with the radio. Drake wouldn't give me time to fix it. He sent it off. I don't know what he told Sam or Randy."

Martin pushed away from the table and walked over to the front window. Joe and Al exchanged looks.

Frank blew smoke. He felt ashamed. "I should've been stronger, I know."

Martin turned from the window. "Forget it Rawlins. What counts now is finding that plane. If the FAA or NTSB doesn't nail Drake's ass to the wall, I will. That piece of chicken shit is going to wish to God he never met me. Nobody has the right to play with people's lives like that. Nobody."

Joe spoke. "If you and Frank can get another plan of action together, I'll line up pilots. Maybe we can get started within a couple of days."

Frank looked at Martin, grateful that the man did not blame him for his weakness. "Hell, I might as well stay. Drake's bound to find out that I paid you a visit. I don't want to work for that SOB anyway. Besides, I want to see first hand what went wrong."

Martin walked to the coat rack and pulled his tan parka off a peg. "And I want to find the only family I have left. Right now, Diana may or may not need me, but sooner or later, I'll bring her home." He zippered his coat. "Come on, Frank." He moved to the door. "You can bunk with me. I'll take care of your expenses. I need your help."

Frank felt relieved to be accepted by Martin. “You got it. For as long as it takes. We’ll find the plane. I know we will.”

Martin opened the door, as Frank retrieved his coat from his chair. He spoke to Joe and Al. “We’ll lay out some more routes over the next few days. I’ll give you a call.” They left the shack.

Joe stood at the doorway and called after them. “I’ll have the guys here Wednesday, ready to go. You can count on it.” Snow blew in his face and chilled him. He shut the door.

CHAPTER 22

Mid morning light filtered through the pine trees. The sky was overcast and although it was cold, it was not snowing. A thin wisp of smoke curled from the chimney of the cabin and disappeared into the grey day. Near the right side of the cabin, the double bit axe was stuck in a tree stump. Stacked neatly beside the makeshift splitting block was a substantial amount of split wood, both fir and deciduous. The ground around the cabin was trampled down with foot activity and a path through the snow led from the cabin porch down to the stream. Several crows cawed in the distance and one answered from a nearby oak tree.

The door to the cabin opened and the crow flew away as Diana stepped off the porch. She walked with a long stride to a nearby pine tree and cut off a small bough section with the hand-axe. Then, went back toward the cabin.

She stopped at the porch steps and turned to look about. She could not believe their luck at finding this place and, although it wasn't much in the way of comfort, she had found a few things that would serve them well. Her exploration of the cabin, the morning after she had sewed up Casey's leg, had yielded a cache of useful items.

The cupboards had a few pots and pans in them and she had discovered a heavy iron fireplace pot on a shelf beneath the skinning table on the left side of the cabin. She had also found some odds and ends of flatware and one paring knife, along with half a dozen tin plates and several tin cups. There were also two other battered metal buckets in the cabin. A half chewed up broom was located underneath the bed. She smiled in the morning light in remembering her ecstasy over discovering those items. But that was over a week ago. Her only disappointment was in not finding any left over cans of food, but that would have been expecting too much.

She went back inside the cabin and noted that Casey was still sleeping. For the first three days after she had sewn up Casey's leg, the woman had barely moved. She had had to help her relieve herself in the one of the two metal buckets that she had found inside the cabin and then promptly get her back in the bed. Casey was weak and at times delirious, but by the sixth day, she appeared much better. The only nourishment that Diana could give her was a heavy dose of pine needle broth and some strips of birch bark to chew on. The bark acted like aspirin and helped to ease Casey's pain.

Diana passed by the bed and stole a quick look at the sleeping face. As she walked to the fireplace she dropped the pine boughs on the table. The fire was warm. She put several more logs on it and then took off her coat. She paused a moment to look at the water in the iron pot which hung over the fire from the wrought iron arm. The water was beginning to steam.

She hung her coat on a peg near the front door and moved back to the table where she began to strip needles from the boughs. She piled the stripped needles onto a ripped cloth which lay in the center of the table. When she had collected a large mound of the green needles, she carefully knotted the cloth, took it to the pot and dropped it in. Within moments, the smell of pine needles permeated the cabin.

Casey stirred. She moaned, but it was not the usual tortured moan that Diana was used to. This one had the sound of life to it.

Diana turned from the fireplace.

"Where are we?" Casey was confused.

Diana moved to the bed and sat down. She took Casey's hands in her own. "Well, it isn't the Holiday Inn, but it's free."

Casey sat up and looked around the cabin. "Ow. Something stuck my butt." She moved the covers aside and saw that the bed was made of pine boughs and mounds of needles.

Diana laughed. "The good thing is they cushion the boards some. The bad thing is if you move wrong they stick you."

"I think I've slept on some beds like this before." Casey smiled. "And, at the Holiday Inn."

Diana laughed. "You're better. No doubt about it." She got up from the bed. "You ready for a continental breakfast?"

Casey was still a little groggy as she swung her legs over the edge of the bed. She gasped when she saw her right thigh. "Oh, God. What happened?" She pulled back the bandage that covered her thigh and gingerly ran her fingers over the scarred area. She looked up at Diana with a worried look on her face.

Diana was holding two cups of steaming broth. "Hey. It's okay. We had a real bad time of it." She sat down next to Casey and handed her a cup. "You fell on the hand-axe. You've been in and out of it for about six days." She put her right arm around Casey.

"I feel weak. I'm hungry." Casey looked into the cup and smelled it. "*Pine Sol*, huh?"

"Yeh, it's all we have so far." Diana got up and went to the table and sat on a wooden chair facing Casey. "I set some snares yesterday, but I haven't had time to check them." She sipped her drink.

Casey stood on shaky legs and steadied herself on the edge of the wooden bed. "Where are my pants? I'm cold."

"Oh, yeh. I had to cut them off of you." Diana went to the shelves underneath the counter and pulled out some of the clothes they had taken from the plane. She found a pair of brown corduroy pants and a flannel blue plaid shirt which she handed to Casey.

"They look kind of big for me."

"Yeh, we've both lost weight."

"Guess I can't be real choosey." She fingered the clothes. She swayed again, still weak.

Diana put her hand on her shoulder. "Like I said before, we need some food. I'll go check the traps." She went to the table and picked up a web made of shoelaces. "I've spent the last few days making new snowshoes and even a sort of fishnet." She proudly showed the net.

Casey just stared at it without expression or comment.

Diana shrugged and moved to the door. She pulled her coat and scarf off the peg and put them on.

Casey sat back down on the bed. "God I hate it here. I want out. I'm useless. I want some food. A bathroom even."

Diana picked up the snowshoes which leaned against the wall. Hunger had made her a little angry and Casey's whining further irritated her. She lashed out.

"Look dammit. I know you've been sick and hurt, but we're here and we can't do anything about it. We're lucky to be alive. That's all I care about. Living. We've survived for almost a month and if we have to wait until spring to get out, then so be it." She slammed out of the cabin.

Casey was silent. She hobbled to the front window and looked outside. She could see Diana plodding toward the stream, the snowshoes flopping through the drifts. She steadied herself on the small window ledge and watched as Diana disappeared into the woods.

Snow was gently falling. Casey turned away from the window and moved to the fireplace.

CHAPTER 23

Diana's face was red from the quick anger that had flashed through her. She pushed past the small pine trees and quickly reached the stream where a newly chopped tree crossed from one bank to the other. She mounted the log in her snowshoes and inched across it sideways to the other side of the creek. She followed a path that she had made in the snow just the day before when she had set out the snares. It made the going easier. As she concentrated on the thought of the snares and what they might hold, she forgot her anger at Casey and even told herself that Casey was right. They should be out of here. And, yes, a bathroom would be nice.

She said aloud, "Actually, a rabbit would be heaven."

The snowfall became heavier as she moved through the woods. She wondered how long she could stay out before the cold and weariness attacked her body. Lack of food had made her weak and her endurance was limited. She came to the first deadfall trap she had set and found it empty, although it was sprung. There were no signs that any animal had been around it.

"Probably a lousy set job on my part. Damn."

She moved off the shallow trail in the snow into some brush. The brush circled a small marshy area and although the ground was frozen, it held a cache of leftover summer plants. Sticking through the snow in low spots were some winter cress and Shepherd's Purse. There were even patches of cranberry, the berries shriveled and frozen. Diana pulled a small cloth bag, which she had made, out of her coat pocket. She stripped the withered foliage from the stems and put them in the bag. She seemed to have added energy as she spotted wild rose bushes along the edge of the marsh. She moved quickly to the rose bushes and pulled the leaves and berries off. The berries would make Rosehip tea and that was ten times better than pine needle tea. Even the cranberries would make a tasty drink. "No more *Pine Sol*, at least, not for a while. That should make Casey perk up." She packed as much of the foliage and berries into the bag as she could and then she saw a stand of birch trees just a little ways away.

The birch trees were near the path that Diana had made the day before and in fact, were near one of the deadfalls that she had set. She did not think about that as she moved to the birch. She reached them and began stripping bark. Diana was unaware that the two wolves which had followed her and Casey from the plane site and several others were now a part of this place and that they had watched her from a distance as she set her traps. They had checked many of them and had already stolen caught rabbits. To her right, the wolves moved silently, approaching another deadfall.

A low growl startled Diana and she looked in the direction toward where the wolves stood. The omega wolf, the lowliest in the pack, grabbed at the deadfall. Diana realized what was happening and she shrieked. "No, dammit. You can't have that. We need it." She yelled and ran toward the wolves.

The omega tried to grab the rabbit again.

Diana was closing the gap. "No. No. Get away." The thought of losing food had caused her to forget all sense of fear. Her screaming caused the wolves to back off a little, but the omega had the rabbit and ran.

Diana was furious, but it was no use. They would not relinquish food and she could yell all she wanted, but it would be merely screaming in the wind. The alpha wolf turned to look back at her and then simply loped off in the direction his mate and the others had gone. He would take the rabbit from the omega and then he and his mate would devour it.

"Damn." Diana uttered a final oath and then turned back to the marshy area. She found some cattails and smiled, for she knew the roots would yield a powdery substance that could be used to make dough, dough for bread. She knelt down in the snow and dug with a knife she had found at the cabin in the half-frozen soil to extract almost two dozen root systems. They were dirty and messy, but she was delighted to have them. Casey was in for a treat.

Diana's anger had vanished and even the loss of the rabbit would not diminish the food she had found that day.

Snow began to fall in even heavier amounts and she finished her cattail harvest abruptly. There would be other times to come back to this marsh. Perhaps, all the time in the world. As she left the area, she decided to check one more trap before returning to the cabin. The trap lay up a slight incline away from the marsh among a stand of fir trees. She saw the trees a short distance away and came to the path she had made yesterday.

As she plodded along, she hoped that the wolves had not found this one. They were a problem, but Diana held a strong belief in the balance of nature and she especially liked the wildness that wolves represented. She had argued with friends over the wolf's right to be a part of the forest, so she would just have to accept it. She muttered aloud, "Hard to be an environmentalist sometimes. Especially now."

The trap was situated under a low limb of a large spruce tree and was hard to spot. Diana wasn't sure which one hid the trap because the snowfall had covered the footsteps made yesterday. She looked under several. Nothing. At her third attempt, not only did she find the trap, but a rabbit had unwarily been recently caught in it. It was still limp and warm.

Diana let out a whoop and a holler, "EEEYOW, yes. Oh, you beautiful bunny, you." She snatched the rabbit out of the trap and stuffed it into her coat pocket. She quickly reset the trap and began to move at almost a run back to the cabin.

When she came to the creek, she stopped long enough to get out of the snowshoes and fairly ran over the log. She was excited to show Casey the food she had snared and also excited that they would finally have something to chew on. She crashed through the small pines and ran to the cabin. As she leaped upon the porch, she shouted, "Casey, Casey, we feast today."

She burst into the cabin and was startled to find Casey standing nude before the fireplace washing herself. A flood of emotion swept through Diana, a mixture of desire for what she saw and of pity for the slender body that was now cut and undernourished. She stumbled backwards. "Excuse me."

Casey in turn was somewhat startled. She pulled a blanket off the chair and covered herself. She also had a mixture of feelings; some she did not understand and would surely never act upon. She looked at Diana and said, "I was terribly dirty. Filthy, in fact. I found some soap and I heated some water." She continued to look directly into Diana's eyes.

Even though they stood a room apart, Diana felt as though Casey's violet eyes could see right into her thoughts and she did not want her to know what she was thinking or how her emotions raged. Finally, embarrassment overcame her when she realized how stupid she must appear standing there with a dead rabbit in her hand. She looked down at it and then back at Casey. The eyes had her. She backed out the door and shut it quietly. She stepped off the porch into the snow and whistled through her teeth, "Sweet Jesus."

CHAPTER 24

Diana stood outside the cabin for a few minutes just looking toward the creek, at the woodpile, at the deer rack and then back at the cabin. Huge flakes of snow landed on her watch cap and on the shoulders of her coat. She could smell the sweet smell of pine wood burning as the smoke wafted from the cabin chimney. The chirping of sparrows and juncos echoed through the woods, occasionally punctuated with the coarse caw of a crow. She thought how easy it would be to stay lost, but then she smiled because she did not believe that she was lost. She wished beyond her wildest hopes, that maybe she had been found. The violet eyes had burned deep within her soul.

A flash of movement by the small pines broke her thoughts. She caught a glimpse of the fleeting alpha wolf as he headed back toward the creek. She called after him, "Well, you won't get this rabbit. He's our dinner."

She lifted the rabbit to look at it and saw how dirty her hands were and she thought how dirty she must be. All the while Casey had been recovering from the cut, Diana had spent the short daylight hours nursing her and making snowshoes and trying to make a fishnet. She had made attempts at cleaning the cabin and chopping wood, but physical weakness caused by little nourishment, made her stop that and she began making dead fall traps. She had not thought about cleaning herself, except for her hands and now, they were filthy again from the morning hunt. She sighed. She felt ashamed of how she must look in the eyes of Casey. She would tend to herself later.

She went to the side of the cabin and laid the rabbit down in the snow and pulled the knife from her pocket. She began the process of skinning the rabbit by cutting its head off. She was in the midst of pulling the skin off when Casey emerged from the cabin.

"Diana. Where are you?"

"Here, by the side." She continued the skinning.

Casey eased herself off the porch and stood at the side, leaning on the logs for support. "Oh. What is that?"

"Lunch, or dinner or whatever." Diana looked up at Casey.

Casey's face was shiny and bright, her hair washed and blond again. The clean flannel shirt and corduroy pants hung loosely on her body. Diana quickly looked back at the task.

"You better go back inside. It's cold out here."

"It feels good to be outside again. I never thought I'd say that, but it does." Snow drifted lazily and landed on her head.

Diana laid the skinned rabbit in the snow and cut a long slash on its stomach down from the top of its neck area to its tail. Blood oozed out of the cut. The gutting had begun. "You might not want to see this."

Casey bit her lip. "You're right. It is cold out here. See you in a bit." She went back into the cabin. She was determined not to throw up.

When Diana had finished the preparation of the rabbit, she washed snow over her hands and then took the throw away parts and left them in the pines. She knew the wolves or a fox or perhaps even a red-tailed hawk would get them and, since she couldn't bury the parts, that was the best way. Maybe they would be so grateful they would leave her traps alone. She smiled. Fat chance of that.

She went inside the cabin. Casey was seated on one of the wooden chairs near the fire, warming herself and running her hands through her hair in an attempt to speed its drying. Diana found it hard not to stare at her. She put the rabbit into a black iron pot that sat on the counter.

Casey turned to her. "All done?"

"Yeh, except for getting some water."

"I'm sorry. I used most of it to wash with."

"Ah, that's okay. I can always get more." Diana pulled the bag containing the leaves and berries out of her coat pocket. She threw it and the strips of birch bark onto the table. "I'll be back in a minute." She grabbed the bucket she used for water and went outside, leaving Casey seated by the fire.

Her abruptness puzzled Casey. It seemed to her that Diana was avoiding her, but why? She remembered that Diana had been angry at her that morning and wondered if she was still angry. Who could say? Diana was so serious about everything. So tense.

She got up from the chair and limped to the table. The strips of birch bark made her remember what Diana had told her. 'Chew it. It acts like aspirin.' She fingered the strips, turning them over and over to study them. The cloth bag Diana had thrown on the table looked full and she wondered what sort of treasures were inside it. Her curiosity got the better of her and when she opened it, all sorts of odd things spilled out, little red shriveled berries, leaves, dirty roots and things that looked like small potatoes. She sniffed at the various items. Some of the leaves and the berries vaguely reminded her of spices or herbs, but she could not place the smells. The roots just smelled like dirt. She could not believe that she might eat any of this.

The door to the cabin opened with a bang and Diana entered carrying a full bucket of water in one hand, and small pine logs in the other. She used her right foot to push the door shut. "Checking out our food?" She set the bucket of water on the table and dropped the logs by the fireplace.

"Just curious. But none of it looks like anything I know."

Diana smiled as she returned from hanging her coat on the peg. As she poured some water into the pot that held the rabbit, she began to talk excitedly.

"We're going to have a great meal. You won't believe this." She picked up the small round tubers. "See these? They're Groundnut tubers. They're just like potatoes. And I found Winter cress and Shepherd's Purse and even some berries to make rosehip tea or even cranberry tea. This is going to be a real feast." She was terribly excited and Casey had to smile.

"Slow down. All we lack are rolls and butter."

Diana was suddenly giddy. "You know what? We do have the makings for bread. Guess how?"

"You found a refrigerator stuffed with *Pillsbury* rolls?"

That remark made Diana laugh. "Not quite, but how about these cat-tail roots? They'll make flour." She picked a root and handed it to Casey.

Casey thought for a moment she was kidding, but Diana looked serious in spite of her laughter. "Flour? You mean like for biscuits?" Casey turned the dirty root over in her hand, and then gave it back to Diana. "I don't believe it. You're kidding."

"No I'm not. Well, sort of. We just have to wash them, then peel off the outer covering. There's a starchy core underneath. You crush the core and soak it in water. The starch settles to the bottom of the container and all you have to do is pour off the water and there's the dough." She smiled.

Casey stared into her eyes and Diana stopped smiling. Those violet eyes, as the song said, gave her '*a total eclipse of the heart.*' Diana looked away.

Casey spoke. "Is there anything I can do to help?"

For a moment, Diana was stunned by the question. Could her face be that transparent? God, she hoped it wasn't. She looked back at Casey and realized that the question was not one of mind reading. It was just an innocent question. She wanted to shriek, "Yes, yes, yes," but prudence and fear made her simply say, "You could wash the tubers and roots for me. I have something I need to do."

Casey smiled. "As long as I can stay here by the fire, I'll be fine."

Diana carried the pot which held the rabbit over to the fireplace and hung it on the iron rod over the fire. She then went to the counter and sneaked a bar of soap and cloth into her pants pocket. "I'll be back shortly." She grabbed her coat and scarf and a bucket and left.

Casey could not imagine what she would do with all these 'things' but Diana had asked her to wash them and she was determined to do her best. She did not want Diana to get angry with her again, at least not over her spoiled attitude. Casey could see that she had a lot to learn about living and as long as she was stuck here, she might as well make the best of it. She had to admit to herself that she had acted spoiled. Maybe her ex-husband had been right all along. No, their problems were deeper than that. Something else had made their marriage go sour, although she never really understood what had happened. In their seven years of marriage, she had never really felt any passion for him and in the end, that took its toll on both of them and they began to spend less and less time with one another. She sighed. Work was her salvation after the split. Work, work, work. Years of work. Now she had no work, "except for these damn things." She cleaned another tuber. "Don't act spoiled," she said aloud. She finished cleaning the small tubers and laid them on the table.

She opened a door on one of the rough wooden cupboards above the counter and found a small amount of all sorts of leaves stacked in little piles. She picked one up and smelled it. It smelled good. She also found a cup that contained a tiny amount of whitish yellow powder that vaguely smelled like flour. She smiled. She saw a smaller pot in the cupboard and decided to try her hand at extracting the 'flour' from the cattail roots. She began the work. After she had washed the roots, she peeled off the outer layer and was surprised to see a white flaky substance. She mumbled aloud, "Good Lord. This is not for real. If my co-workers at the ad agency could see this, they'd die laughing. Cattail bread." She put the peeled, crushed roots into the small pot of water and watched for a moment as the white flakes settled to the bottom.

The aroma of the rabbit cooking in the pot drifted through the room. Casey took the small groundnut tubers and dropped them in the iron pot with the rabbit. It smelled okay, but could she eat it? Her stomach told her that she was hungry, but her eyes would still see a rabbit when it came time to eat. This was not going to be easy.

She had no idea what to do with the recent cache of leaves that Diana had found, so she just let them lay on the table. Her work was done. She hobbled to the front window and looked outside. She saw Diana coming through the pines near the creek, headed for the cabin. Her brown curly hair was wrapped in her scarf. Even from a distance, Casey could see that Diana had scrubbed her face and washed her hair. As she came, she swung the bucket in a circle and sang. Casey could not clearly hear the words, but she thought she heard *'eclipse of the heart.'* It made no sense to her, so she walked back to the table and waited for Diana.

CHAPTER 25

Martin stood near the rear window of his motel room and looked outside at the gently falling snow. He listened intently into the telephone, merely nodding his head and saying, "Uh, huh." The clouds parted and the setting sun turned the sky a hot pink. Shafts of sunlight slanted through the window and across the room. Martin moved to one bed and sat down.

Frank sat on the other bed closest to the door and smoked. He watched Martin's face.

Martin spoke into the phone, "Look Drake the weather is breaking up a little and some of the guys are willing to start searching again. We need your help."

He listened to Drake and then said, "Yeh, I'm sure you told the Feds everything you could, but maybe they're missing something. I spent most of my time in Nam finding downed planes. The Feds might not put two and two together. This is important to me."

He paused again, listening to Drake. He winked at Frank.

"Sure, I know how insurance companies operate. That's all the more reason to come up here and look at the charts. That way you can tell everyone that you're doing everything possible to find it."

Martin spent several more minutes convincing Carl Drake to come up to Wisconsin. He flattered him by seeming to understand Carl's predicament, "You deserve some time away from all the harassment. I know what jerks those feds can be. They're always trying to make the little guy look bad."

Apparently that speech got to Carl, because Martin broke into a wide grin and gave Frank a thumb up signal. Frank chuckled. Finally, Martin gave directions on how to find a local steak house and arranged a meeting time. The phone call came to a conclusion.

"Yep, see you a week from Thursday. Bye." Martin hung up.

Frank put out his cigarette. "So the son of a bitch is actually going to come."

Martin nodded.

"Damn I'd love to see his face if he knew I'd been talking to you." He picked up a glass of *7-Up* from the nightstand and swirled the ice around before he took a drink.

Martin paced about the room, slapping his right fist into his open left hand.

"You'll get to see the son of a bitch after I've had time to set him up for the kill. It's a dark place. He won't expect you to be there."

"Damn I can hardly wait. This is going to be fun."

"You can sit at the bar and wait until I give you a signal to join us."

Frank took another drink. "Don't make me sit at the bar too long. I can only take so much *7-Up*. Straight that is, if you know what I mean."

Martin smiled. "You're doing fine pal. You got the whiskey devil beat." He grabbed his coat off the rack. "Let's go have some spaghetti and milk. What do you say?"

Frank set his glass down and grabbed his coat. "Sounds good to me."

They walked out into the cold night air. Overhead the stars were beginning to shine brighter as the evening light faded and swiftly turned the heavens to a navy blue. A sliver of a new moon raced with the passing clouds, while the misty shadow image of its larger self pursued the passage of seasons.

CHAPTER 26

Time has a way of beginning and ending all things, of making the new grow familiar and comfortable and of revealing the unexpected pleasures in the simple everyday process of living. So it was at the cabin in the wilds of Wisconsin.

Within the short passage of another week, Casey had come from the edge of possible death for a second time and now stood on firm legs and felt the strength begin to return to her undernourished body. The wound had healed and although an unwanted scar remained, she began to realize how fortunate she had been to survive. She had never been religious, but something within her recognized that a greater power had watched over her. She felt humbled and began to understand that somehow she was really a part of this wilderness. The skyline of Chicago seemed further and further away. Some days she never even missed it. Other days she did. Diana had given her the gift of a journey toward self-reliance and for that she was grateful. But, inwardly, she trembled. And whatever was happening inside her caused her to struggle more and more with the bond that was growing between her and Diana because there were parts that she did not understand. And, feelings for Diana that were foreign to her. Her dreams were filled with odysseys of journeys through deserts, across storm-laden seas and snow capped summits. Animals prowled the jungles of her mind and chased her relentlessly. Fear mingled with wild passion. Quite often a lion or a wolf morphed into Diana and the chase ended. When that happened, Casey was both relieved and yet, oddly, fear still gripped her heart. She did not understand. It was in just such a dream that she slept.

Early morning sun found its way through the pines and the changing axis of the earth made the rays penetrate the cold and the snow began to recede and melt. The slow dripping of snow from the roof, at least for now, had begun.

Diana slept beside Casey. Her sleep was tormented with waking and drifting. She heard all sorts of noises. This morning, the constant drip of water awakened her. She lay on her back, and listened to the methodical drip, drip, drip. Then there was another sound, unexpected, but vaguely familiar. She sat up and listened intently. It was a scratching sound and it came from the front door. She looked at Casey and saw that she still slept. She carefully eased out bed and tiptoed to the door of the cabin.

The scratching came again. Diana jerked the door open and was startled to see the male alpha wolf standing there holding a dead limp rabbit between its jaws.

The sudden door opening also startled the wolf and he dropped the rabbit at Diana's feet. He jumped off the porch and ran to the tree near the deer rack, then turned and looked back at her. He sat down on his haunches and stared in her direction. Diana was perplexed. When she knelt down and picked up the dead furry creature, the wolf merely sat and looked at her. She stared back at him. Finally, the wolf loped away into the forest. Diana watched him go until she could see him no more.

As she closed the cabin door, she said aloud, "Well, I'll be damned."

The cool air from the open door had awakened Casey. She asked, "Who are you talking to?"

"You won't believe what just happened. I've heard stories about things like this, but I just figured it came from people suffering from cabin fever."

"Have you lost your mind? What's going on?" Casey was dismayed by the dumbfounded look on Diana's face.

Diana approached the bed and held the rabbit up for Casey to see. "This is what I'm talking about. The wolf brought it. Just like a pet dog or cat brings the catch of the day to lay at the master's doorstep."

"Are you telling me the wolf gave us this food?"

"Yeh. That's what I'm saying. I saw him do it. I don't believe it, but I saw it."

"You're serious." Casey studied Diana's face because one thing she had discovered about Diana was her delight in playing tricks. She had been caught many times in Diana's teasing jokes.

"Don't try to fool me. I'm on to you."

Diana smiled. "That's the one bad thing about crying wolf. Sometimes it backfires." She gave Casey her most serious look. "Really, the wolf did give us this."

Casey shook her head. "God, Diana, if I ever get out of here, the stories I'll have to tell will top any that are told at the agency Christmas party."

"I wouldn't tell this one. People will think you went deliriously berserk."

"Why would the wolf do that?"

"Like I said, it's like a pet sometimes does. It's a form of respect. Acceptance."

Casey looked out the window and then back at Diana. "I don't know if I'll ever understand any of this."

Diana fingered the rabbit. "I see the wolves all the time when I'm out checking the traps. Sometimes when I'm out, I go to the bathroom. As crass as it sounds, I've seen the wolf sniff where I urinated. He knows my scent. And, probably yours. They've decided to let us in their territory, I guess." Diana rose from the bed and went to the counter where she laid the rabbit.

They were silent for a moment. Then Casey pulled herself out of bed. Like Diana, she was wearing a large flannel shirt and wool socks. She saw that her shirt and socks were dirty.

"I think I'll bathe this morning, maybe try to wash some clothes. Are you going out on the traps?"

Diana had been staring out the side window. "Later. I'm going down to the creek now. It's running free in some spots; particularly by the big rock." She picked up a bar of soap and her brush from the counter. She stooped to put on her boots.

"Aren't you putting your pants on?"

"No. Just throw me a blanket."

Casey gave her a puzzled look, but tossed her one of the small airline blankets.

"See you in a bit." Diana wrapped the blanket around her shoulders and left.

Casey went to the door and yelled after her. "I'll skin the rabbit."

Diana turned around and smiled. "Right on, pilgrim." She disappeared through the pines and headed for the big rock.

Casey shut the door and moved to the window on the right side of the cabin. She knew she could see the big rock from that vantage point and sure enough, Diana emerged from behind the small pines. She could see her plainly as she leaped on the flat surface of the boulder which jutted out into the stream. Casey did not know why she was watching Diana; she just knew that she wanted to. She watched as Diana dropped the blanket and then removed her clothes. She saw her step from the rock into the stream and totally submerge. Then Diana popped up and quickly lathered her body and hair with the soap. Casey stood transfixed, watching. Diana submerged once more and pulled herself up onto the rock and sat nude on the blanket, brushing her hair.

Streaks of morning sun filtered through the barren trees and seemed to cast a glow on the white body that Casey watched. She could plainly see the rounded breasts, the muscled arms, and the lithe legs and the curly brown hair. And across the creek, Casey saw the wolf also watching Diana. Diana seemed to see the wolf, but did not react or seem to care that he watched.

Casey could not take her eyes off the woman. What was happening to her? Then she saw Diana stand up and look toward the cabin as she pulled the blanket around her body. Casey quickly moved away from the window.

In the fireplace, the burning embers crackled and sizzled. Casey's face and loins were on fire as she moved toward the back of the cabin and past the bed.

CHAPTER 27

The full moon shone brightly on the little town. The streets were almost empty, except for an occasional pick-up truck or 4x4 that snaked its way to neon lit bars and taverns that made up Hayward's nightlife. The snow that had inundated the landscape for the past month was daily giving way to the warming sun. In the melting of the day, puddles of brown water dotted the dirt parking lots of the bars, by night thin crusts of ice belied the slush that laid underneath, waiting for the unwary.

Carl Drake steered his pale blue Lincoln into the alley and to the parking lot behind the bar. The wheels slung slush as they broke through the layers of ice and the moon danced on the shattered shards. Carl braked his car, cut the engine and the lights. He stepped out and his heavy weight crunched through the ice. "Shit," he cursed as he moved his stubby cigar around in his mouth. He looked down at his wet, muddy *Tony Llama* boots. "It's a goddamn mine field out here." Careful as he tried to be, he stepped on another 'mine' and his other foot broke through. Curses ricocheted off the tiny brick buildings as he made his way to the tavern entrance.

Martin sat near the doorway at a square wooden table in the dimly lit bar and grill and nursed a draft beer. On the table were several charts. A scattering of people were in that area eating and drinking while others were in another room dancing to the strains of country western. The aroma of char-grilled steaks saturated the bar. Martin's chair faced the doorway.

The door banged open and even before he saw Carl, the smell of food was obliterated by the scent of a vintage *Macanudo* cigar as the smoke wafted through the room. The hairs on the back of Martin's neck tingled.

Carl's muddy boots thumped on the worn wooden floor as he crossed to where Martin sat. He extended his hand.

Martin stood to greet him. "Glad you could make it."

Drake tossed his coat on a chair and sat down to the left of Martin, his back to the bar. He looked around. "Damn it's dark in here." He took a final drag on the *Macanudo*.

"Sure is. How was the trip?"

"Smooth sailing, except for the damn parking lot."

Martin sipped his beer and said nothing.

The silence bothered Carl. He laid his cigar stub in the ashtray.

"Like I told you on the phone, I want to find the ship as bad as you do. Hell, those insurance people are driving me nuts."

Martin nodded and continued to sip beer while he studied Drake's face.

Drake fidgeted, then reached inside his coat pocket and pulled out several cigars. He laid one on the table.

"Mind if I smoke?"

"No, sure go ahead."

Drake looked down at the charts. "Well, I see you're all set to run the search again." He looked around the room and said loudly, "If I could get a damn waitress over here, I'd have a drink and we could get down to business."

Martin looked up at the bartender. An older waitress moved off a bar stool and came to the table to face Carl.

Drake lit his cigar. "Glad you could make it honey. Give me a double scotch, straight up. Oh, and don't give me no cheap stuff, see. He's buying." Carl laughed as he blew smoke.

The waitress smiled sweetly, "Sure thing, honey. I can see you're a man of class."

She addressed Martin, "Need another?"

"Not yet. In about ten minutes, maybe."

The waitress left.

Drake began to feel at ease. "So what's the story?"

Martin unfolded the charts and spread them out on the table.

"You can see by the crossed off areas that we've covered a lot of territory in the last six weeks. It just doesn't make sense that they'd have been so far off course. We're stumped."

"They were supposed to fly Victor 129. Sam knew that by heart. I've been all over that with the feds." He blew a large puff of smoke as the waitress returned with his drink.

Martin continued. "I'm sure, but it's like the pieces don't fit."

Drake took a swig of his drink. "What are you drivin' at?"

"Is it possible that something could have been screwy with the nav system?"

Carl nervously fidgeted with his necktie. "Anything's possible. All I know is that the ship was in top notch condition." He took a large gulp of scotch. "Sure, there was a slight problem with the radio before the flight left, but I had one of our mechanics go over it and he gave it a clean bill of health."

Martin had him. "So you're saying that the ship was okay before takeoff?"

Carl blew a billowing cloud of smoke. "You're damn right, pal. Say, I wouldn't let one of my planes go anywhere if it wasn't in perfect shape."

Martin motioned toward the bar and Carl followed the gesture. Frank moved toward the table and into the light.

Carl saw him. "Hey, what the hell is this?"

Martin calmly said, "This is Frank Rawlins, pal. Remember him?"

Carl pushed away from the table and stood up, his face angry.

Martin got up quickly and pushed Carl back into his seat.

"Sit down, Pal, and finish your drink."

Drake looked up at Frank. "You're supposed to be on a vacation. Well, you got a permanent one now lush head. You're fired." He finished his drink in one gulp and slammed the glass down on the table.

Frank plopped a *7-Up* can on the table and sat down to Carl's left. "You got three things wrong. First, I'm not on vacation. Second, I'm not a lush head anymore. And three, you can't fire me. I quit. You just struck out."

They had him hemmed in. He looked at Martin belligerently. "So what's the deal?" He blew smoke.

Martin spoke quietly. "The deal is, you tell me about the airplane and I won't smash your face. Is that simple enough for you?"

"Say, where do you get off comin' out with these cheap threats?"

Martin was furious now. He grabbed Drake's necktie and choked him with it as he pulled his face within inches of his own. "This isn't any cheap threat, you lousy lying son of a bitch. I know all about your messing with the maintenance records. My girl was on that crate and if I don't find it pretty soon, you have my word, I'll make you wish to God that you had gone down with it."

Drake managed a strangled cough.

Martin's blue eyes flashed with controlled rage as he released his grip on the necktie.

"Now, what do you know about the nav system in that plane?"

Drake sputtered and twisted his tie around and away from his neck. He was clearly angry, but he also was afraid of Martin.

"Take it easy, I'll tell you what I know." He twisted his neck sideways several times, then continued, "One of the pilots said that the system seemed to be giving a false magnetic heading."

Martin squinted his eyes. "Like what?"

"Like it could have been off maybe ten degrees."

Frank's eyes widened. "Ten degrees? Why in the hell would you let the plane…?"

Drake interrupted him. "Shut up souse head. You're done, Remember?" With that said, Carl stood up. "And I'm done too. I ain't sayin' nothin' else." He stubbed out his cigar.

Martin jumped up. "For once you're right." He slugged Carl flat in the mouth.

There was stunned look on Drake's face and then he fell backwards, knocked out cold. Martin picked up a wrapped cigar that was left on the table and stuffed it in Carl's mouth.

The waitress came over to the table with a drink tray which held Martin's second drink. She looked at Carl and then at Martin.

He smiled. "I told this guy this was a non smoking section. He just wouldn't listen to reason." He threw some money on the table. "When he comes to, use this money to buy him a dinner. Then tell him if we see his sorry ass in town tomorrow, Frank and I plan on whipping it until both of us drop from exhaustion."

The waitress smiled at Martin. "You must be reformed smokers. Most people don't get that crazy over a little smoke." She looked at Drake again, then back to Martin. "You want your drink, honey?"

Martin took the drink off the tray. "No, I've had enough. Drake looks like he could use one though." He poured the drink on Carl's face. Carl never moved.

Frank picked the charts up off the table. "Well, buddy. You pack one hell of a whollop. I'll just have to wait. I won't hit a man when he's down and out." Frank laughed as he and Martin donned their coats and left the bar.

They hooted and hollered loudly, as they hop scotched through the alley to the parking lot trying to avoid the watery potholes, then climbed into Martin's rented *Bronco* and rode off into the cool moonlit night, happy, like two young cowboys who had just scored at Ruby's brothel. Long after the taillights of the vehicle had vanished into the night, their laughter continued to echo off the store fronts of the all but deserted small town. The neon signs blinked and winked.

The potholes refroze and waited.

CHAPTER 28

The same full moon that illuminated the night at Hayward, danced off the flowing water of the creek by the cabin. An owl glided silently through the maze of barren tree branches, landed on a large sycamore and gazed out over the land with eyes alert for any movement. It hooted. Somewhere in the distance another hooted. The wolf and his mate stood by the stream drinking the cold water. Their eyes also alert for any movement.

Inside the cabin, the fireplace glowed with the incineration of logs that were stacked high inside the stone hearth. Diana and Casey were seated across from one another at the table enjoying an evening meal of rabbit and groundnut tubers, along with copious amounts of rosehip tea laced with liquor. In the center of the table was a container of cattail tops and some other dried weeds that Casey had arranged into a bouquet. Over half a dozen of the miniature liquor bottles they had brought from the plane were lined up on one side of the table. All, but one of them were empty.

Casey raised her tin cup. "I propose a toast."

Diana smiled as she raised her tin cup. "Hear. Hear."

Casey continued, "I salute your competitive spirit and your willingness to offer shelter and food to a foreigner in this land."

Diana felt giddy and all she could do was laugh. "Yes."

Casey went on, "I salute brother wolf, who has taught me how to mark my territory..."

Diana burst into gales of laughter.

"Now don't interrupt; this is serious."

Diana put on a serious smiling face.

Casey said, "and I salute him for not eating us."

Diana interjected, "Don't forget the rabbit." She waved her left hand over the plates of rabbit bones that lay before them.

Casey put on a feigned serious look. "I was getting to that."

She cleared her throat. "I salute brer rabbit, who has willingly given us sustenance while we grew strong in body and renewed our faith in ourselves. I salute the trees and the creek and the cattails and pine needles…"

Diana was beside herself with laughter. "Casey, stop. That's enough. Our drinks will evaporate before you're done."

Casey clinked Diana's cup and stood up. "Okay." Her eyes turned softly serious as she looked directly into Diana's eyes.

"Then this final salute."

Diana sensed a change in Casey and she stood up facing those devastating violet eyes.

Casey looked at her without blinking. "I salute you, lady, for showing me that life is more beautiful than I had ever imagined. I salute this place, knowing in my heart that I could stay here with you forever, even though I know that that wish is impossible." She downed her drink.

Diana downed hers. "I'd like to make a toast." She reached for the remaining single bottle of liquor and poured half into Casey's cup and half into hers. She raised her cup.

Casey met her gaze.

Diana spoke softly, trying to control the hidden emotion that lay within her heart.

"I salute you, Casey, for teaching me to laugh and to see the softer side of who I am. I salute where we are, knowing in my heart that I could stay here with you forever, even though I know it's impossible." She paused for a moment. "I salute the seasons of our years and the seasons of our lives and I finally accept the seasons of the heart. You may never understand that, but it is something you taught me and for that I am grateful."

They stood facing one another silently and without moving for what seemed to each of them as an eternity, looking deeply into the other's heart and soul. Then they touched their cups together and downed their drinks.

The violet eyes eclipsed Diana's heart and she placed her cup on the table. She backed away and moved to get her coat from the peg.

Casey watched as Diana went outside into the moonlit night. She did not want her to go, but she did not know how to say what was in her heart. She finally had admitted the truth to herself, but she did not have the courage to tell Diana. She stood silently as the door creaked shut.

A slight errant wind whistled through the pine trees. Mourning doves cooed softly to one another as Diana stepped off the porch and into the snow. She looked skyward at the stars and saw the flash of a burning asteroid as it streaked earthward.

The fire that burned within her soul was out of control and she did not know how much longer she could contain it. Old wounds, scars and fears no longer served in extinguishing the desire she felt for Casey. She would not act upon those desires. She couldn't. She wouldn't. She was not sure how Casey felt.

She pushed through the small pines and made her way to the large rock in the creek. She accomplished the short leap from land to rock easily and stood on it gazing into the water. Above the murmuring sound of the stream, she heard movement on the other side. The wolf exited from a small stand of firs and into view in the moonlight. He stared at Diana.

Diana stared back at him and then spoke. "Well, brother wolf, what can you tell me now? How am I to survive without a heart?"

The lone wolf moved a few paces. A smaller wolf came from the firs and took her place at the side of the male alpha. They both watched Diana.

"Ah, I see. You also have problems with your heart. You and I are truly brothers."

Behind her, the creaking of the cabin door startled the wolves and they moved back into the shadow of the fir trees. Diana turned toward the cabin and saw the silhouette of Casey standing in the doorway, wrapped in a blanket.

Casey called softly. "Diana. Diana, come to bed." She dropped the blanket and in the glow from the fireplace behind her form, Diana could see that Casey stood nude.

"Sweet Jesus." Diana whispered. "I am undone."

Casey moved away from the door, leaving it open.

A gentle wind rustled the pines. The doves cooed and the smell of burning wood drifted through the moonlit sky. The owl listened to the footsteps that crunched through the snow and then heard the footfall upon the wooden porch. He flew off through the trees before he heard the creaking of the closing cabin door.

CHAPTER 29

❦

Time drifted by in a haze of lovemaking that left Diana and Casey exhausted and yet somehow exhilarated. As weeks passed, the wild passion that they had felt for one another subsided like the melting snow of the season and in its place, an awakening of peace and contentment passed over them. They reveled in the sprouting of grass along the banks of the stream and they delighted in the sound of the ever-increasing chatter and chirping of the birds who had returned north. Everything around them had come to life.

For Casey, the woman who had lost herself in the canyons of the city, the discovery of life, unfettered and running wild, had awakened another soul within her being. She felt free at last. She dug her bare toes in the patches of soil dried by March winds and watched the skies for the vee shape of geese as they headed northward toward Canada. She helped Diana dig cattail roots and made little biscuits with the flour. She had learned how to set traps and skin rabbits and how to find watercress and groundnut tubers. She had lost her fear of this wild place. She was almost whole again. But not quite.

Casey's face had lost its worried look, but in her heart there was a fear that even she could not tell Diana. For as long as this would last or could last, she would hold on and take in all that was around her. She loved Diana more than anyone she had ever loved before, and probably more than she ever would again, but she feared the consequences of that love. Diana seemed to have no fears. But Casey was not in that place and so, she did not speak of the dark shadow that was in her heart.

For her part, Diana was feeling the old sensation of falling in love again, except this time it was somehow different. Casey had aroused a level of passion mixed with a sense of caring that Diana had never experienced before. She took Diana to places in their lovemaking that Diana never thought she would ever go, with nights of love so intense that Diana struggled to keep from weeping with joy. She wanted to devour this woman who had stolen her soul and eclipsed her heart. Slowly her fears of old, those of betrayal and loss vanished and she gave herself totally and unconditionally to Casey. She did not say so to Casey, but she knew it had happened. Perhaps she would never tell her, because part of Diana still could not believe that this time it might just be for a lifetime.

She was not sure how committed Casey was to her. Diana had learned from other loves that commitment was a continuous job that demanded the willingness to love without reservation or regrets or judgments. Diana understood that part, but she also knew that temptations as easy as the next bed partner could destroy relationships that did not weather betrayal. She had been on both sides of betrayal and it had cost her dearly. She had learned to never say never when it came to affairs of the heart. She hoped that this time, it was a forever commitment. She wanted it to be. With her whole heart.

And, so the days passed.

By the second week of March, several days of fifty-degree weather had melted the snow to the vanishing point. Only little snatches of snow remained under the fir trees or along the north side of the incline that bordered the creek near the cabin. The land around the cabin and down to the creek was blessedly devoid of snow. There was an old familiar smell to the air that could only be described as a spring smell—moist and warm and somehow clean and new.

Most mornings, Diana arose shortly after sun-up. She loved to go for short walks, to inspect the changes that were occurring in and around the cabin. Sometimes Casey went with her, but mostly, Casey slept a little later. Diana did not mind, for she knew that Casey had come through a very traumatic time and that the wound, although healed, had taken its toll on her, mainly because they were without enough food for so long. Now it was different, but it would take time for Casey to regain her full strength.

This morning, Diana left Casey still sleeping and made her way to the stream. She carried the small net made from shoelaces that she had started making when they first found the cabin over a month ago. Then, it was busywork. Now it was business. She was determined to catch a fish. If she could, it would be their first. She inspected the net, as she moved through the small pines near the creek. She spoke to the net. "Do your job. I'm tired of rabbit."

She went toward the rock, knowing that a deep pool lay on the outer edge of the rock, but that a smaller pool also lay between the rock and the shore. Yesterday, while bathing in the stream, she had spotted trout in the smaller pool. Today, she would have one.

Diana stopped short of the rock and got down on her hands and knees and inched to the edge of the creek bank. She laid down flat. Her flannel shirt was little protection from the dampness of the soil, but it was not cold. She rolled up her right sleeve and slowly put her hand, which held the net, into the water. She peered cautiously into the pool. Several trout were swimming in circles. She inched further out, making slow deliberate moves.

The pines behind rustled. Casey said, "What the heck are you doing?"

"Shhh. Quiet."

Casey knelt down. She whispered, "What is it.?"

"I'm trying to catch a fish."

Casey was amused. "Sure you are." She kissed Diana's neck and ran her hand inside her shirt to cup her breast.

"Sweet, Jesus, Casey. I'm serious." Shivers ran through Diana.

"Woman does not live by bread alone."

Diana wiggled away from Casey's touch. "And woman does not live by love alone."

Casey kept teasing. "Neither one of us has to be alone anymore."

Diana stopped her fishing and rolled over to look at Casey. She studied her face.

"Maybe you'd say that to any person you were stranded with for months."

"No, I wouldn't. Besides, you're not any person. You're the woman I love and I never thought I'd say that. I never thought I'd fall in love with a woman."

Diana inched her hand and net back into the water. "Surprised, huh? Well, there are plenty of Girl Scouts out there. Maybe even some in Chicago."

She seemed to study the water, but looked at Casey's reflection.

Casey smiled. "Perhaps, but I want your cookies not theirs."

Diana jerked around at that tease and then realized that a fish had just gotten into the net.

"Jesus, jenny. I got one! I got one!" She jerked her hand out of the water and a foot long trout was trapped in the webbing of the net.

Casey was stunned.

Diana flipped the net on the ground and trapped the fish between her two hands. "Get me a rock, quick."

Casey jumped up and ran a little ways up stream to get a rock. She ran back. "What's this for?"

"To kill the fish, of course. Give it to me."

"Oh, Diana, do you have to do that?"

Diana stopped and looked up at Casey. The violet eyes pleaded. "If I don't, it will die anyway. I've touched it roughly."

"Are you sure?" Casey knelt down to look at the speckled trout.

"Yeh, Casey. I'm sure. If you had said how you felt sooner, I could have released it in the water."

Casey touched the side of the fish. "It's smooth."

"Casey, it's a fish. It will taste better than a rabbit. Okay? If you don't want me to catch others, I won't. Only this one will not make it if I put it back. Honest."

Casey looked at Diana. "I guess I'm being silly. It's just that love has made me not want to hurt anything."

Diana still held the fish securely between her hands. "I know. We can go back to civilization and order fish in a fancy restaurant and pretend we didn't hurt it."

Casey was stung. "I didn't mean it that way. Kill your fish. You earned it."

An argument, and so early. Diana wanted not to argue. "The point is, Casey, we need it. All of this is beautiful, but everything has its time and its place. I'm not just killing to kill. This is our food. I thought you'd like trout for breakfast."

Casey held Diana's look with her violet eyes. "I would like trout for breakfast. I don't know why I got sentimental. Testy."

"Is there something else going on inside you?"

"No." She lied. "No. Teach me how to catch a fish."

She handed Diana the rock.

"If you're serious, I will." Diana took the rock and hit the wiggling trout hard between the eyes. She hit it again and it lay still. A small trickle of blood oozed out from the blow.

Casey had looked away on the first blow, but watched the second one. "Tell me something Diana. Remember when I ate the whole candy bar and you told me that you'd kill me if I tried to get your share? Did you mean it?"

"I meant it then, because I loved myself more than you. Now I would give you all my food, if you asked." Diana removed the fish from the net. "I'm going back to the cabin." Diana started to get up.

Casey reached out and stopped her. "Teach me to catch a fish, Diana. I want to catch one for you."

There was something sensuous about the way Casey looked at her and Diana had to fight the urge to leap upon her. She sensed that something else was going on in Casey's mind, but she did not have any idea what. She said,

"All right." She knelt back down on the bank and picked up the net and handed it to Casey.

"Lie flat along side the bank."

Casey did as instructed.

Diana put her arm across Casey's shoulder and moved her hand along her arm.

"Put the net in the water underneath the cut out area next to the bank. Don't move your hand and just let the net flow out with the current."

"How will I know if any fish are near?"

"Watch closely for a flash of silver. That's the underbelly of the fish as it turns. When you see the flash, you'll know they're looking at your hand. Move slowly and pull the net real slow. They swim right into it." Diana stood up.

Casey peered into the water. "I think I can do it."

"You can, it just calls for directed activity that's all."

Diana started through the pines.

Casey called after her. "I'll catch one for you, you'll see. Make sure you wait. I'd like to have breakfast in bed."

Diana was caught in mid-stride, "Sweet, Jesus." She blew air between her lips. Then she continued toward the cabin. The fish dangled from her hand. She did not want this to ever end.

Overhead and far away, she heard the faint sound of an engine. She went inside the cabin and could not hear anything except the beating of her heart.

CHAPTER 30

Martin Forrester banked the single engine Cessna 152 to the left and flew low over the forest. He peered down, intent on finding the downed craft. He felt like he was back in Nam, looking for needles in haystacks. For months, the downed plane had eluded all efforts to find it, first due to weather, but mostly due to Drake's lies and his cover-up and doctoring of records. The areas that had been crossed off the maps and charts were larger and he felt more secure in having crossed off some, no need to double check anymore. "Where are we now, buddy?"

Frank sat to Martin's right, holding charts and trying to juggle a can of pop. He took a drink. "We're almost due east of Hayward about twenty five miles. I think we're over Ashland County, but it's not easy to match aerials with county maps."

He put the pop can between his knees.

Martin asked, "Are we still near the Moose River?"

Frank looked at a chart, peered outside and then looked back at the aerial. "Naw. That's a little north. That stream down there is Black Creek." Then he added, "I think." He looked back outside again. Then jerked excitedly and strained to look behind him.

Martin sensed excitement, "What is it?"

"Do a one eighty. I just saw a flash of silver. I'm positive I did. This could be it." Frank craned his neck, straining to see the flash again.

Martin was excited now. He began the bank to the right.

"I don't see it. Where?"

"Keep rotating. I know I caught a flash. What else could it be out here?"

Martin continued the rotation of the small plane.

Frank yelled, "There! There it is! By God, we found it!"

"I see it. Oh, my God! It's in the middle of nowhere. There's no road. Nothing."

Martin banked the plane in a tight rotation and the wing tip rotated around the crash site. Trees had been shattered and the debris covered the craft, but parts of it were visible. He was surprised to see that the right half of the fuselage had survived the impact. He knew from experience that the pilot had tried to spare that side of the plane, so that some might live.

Frank said, "I don't see any movement, but holy smokes. Somebody built a shelter."

Martin had been so intent on looking at the craft that he had not seen the makeshift lean-to. He looked at an area near a craggy rock and saw the shelter.

"It has to be Diana. It has to be." He grabbed the mike from the clip. "Hayward Unicom. This is Charlie five niner seven. We have a location on the craft. Over."

"Charlie five niner seven, this is Al at Hayward. Whadda ya got? Over."

"Hayward, we have a smashed up aircraft approximately twenty five miles east of Hayward. About five miles south of Moose River. We can see a creek. We think it's Black Creek. Over."

"Five niner seven, Joe's working on the location. Are you returning? Over."

Martin looked at Frank and yelled above the engine noise, "I hope the Feds aren't monitoring." He then spoke into the mic.

"Hell, no, Hayward. I'm going down and take a look. Over and out." He replaced the mic back on its bracket and turned off the radio.

Frank looked the area over. "That field near the plane looks okay, but it could be mushy."

Martin extended the flight path away from the crash and then did a one eighty turn back into the wind in preparation to land. He dropped all the flaps he could.

"Hang on Frank; I'm going to set 'er down. I have to know if Diana made it. What do you think?"

"I think you'll drop in no matter what I say. Go for it. You've waited a long time for this. Just do it."

Martin smiled broadly as he flared out for a soft, short field landing. The plane came down at a steep angle to skim over treetops and then sunk quickly toward the ground. He pulled back on the yoke and the nose rose up and the Cessna's tricycle gear hit on the back two wheels. Then as it slowed down on the bumpy sod, Martin eased the nose gear down. They rolled to a stop just short of the pine bough arrow that Diana and Casey had made over two months ago.

Martin cut off the engine. "Hell hardly sunk in at all. We'll get out easy." He opened the door. "Now let's go check it out."

Frank crawled out on the other side and approached the pine boughs on the ground. "Geez, Martin, I couldn't see it from the air, but look, this is an arrow. Hell, it would have shown in the snow easy."

They both looked in the direction in which it pointed.

Martin moved away from the arrow and headed to the shelter.

"That arrow and this shelter could only have been made by Diana. I know her work. She's alive, Frank. God bless it, she's alive." Tears welled in his eyes.

Frank slapped him on the back. "Let's take a look at the wreck." He began to walk toward the plane and got within thirty feet of it and stopped dead in his tracks. "Oh, my God. The smell."

The stench of rotting flesh overpowered him. He covered his nose with his hand and dug into his pocket for a handkerchief.

Martin stopped alongside him. He covered his nose with his hand. "Damn, it's bad."

Frank moved backwards. "Martin, I'm sick."

"Give me your handkerchief. I've seen this before. No need for you to go in. Go check on the arrow."

"I'm sorry. I just never handled anything like this." He gave Martin his handkerchief and backed away another ten feet.

"It's okay. I understand. I won't be able to take if for long, but I have to know for sure about Diana. I know she built the shelter, but it doesn't tell me where she is now."

Frank watched as Martin climbed up into the shattered aircraft and then he turned and walked toward the direction the arrow pointed and headed up the incline. He stopped at the top of the hill and looked back toward the commercial plane. It was surprisingly intact, but he understood now why they could not find it. Trees hid a large part of it even now and he could imagine that when there had been snow any part that was not hidden by broken pines, would have been covered by the snow. "Damn. It was really hidden."

Frank turned toward the woods and noticed the notches on the trees. He followed them for a time and was amazed at how high off the ground the marks seemed to be. It couldn't have been Diana. He remembered her as being only five and a half feet tall. Then it occurred to him that the snow must have been very deep and that whoever made them might not have been very tall at all. He smiled. Martin did know his daughter all right.

The woods were alive with bird songs and of all sorts of leaves and grasses growing in the awakening earth. The forest was beautiful and it seemed to Frank that it was easy walking. He had no trouble at all in following the chopped notches. As he approached a stand of fir trees and some large oak, he heard the sound of buzzing. It was loud. His gaze followed the sound downward to the ground and he saw a dark figure with what seemed like thousands of Blue bottle flies swarming around it. The rot of death assailed his nostrils. He crooked his elbow, covered his nose and mouth with his sleeved arm and then held his breath. He moved forward quickly to get a look at the figure. He couldn't be sure, but he thought it was a man. He saw that the notches continued beyond the body. Frank had seen enough. The noise from the huge blue flies was deafening. He swatted at them and ran back the way he had come.

When he had gotten far enough away from the body, he stopped to lean against a tree and to light a cigarette. He wanted to rid his senses of the smell.

Frank leaned against the tree for a moment and looked around him. The woods were coming to life, both with the living and with the dying. He had not found a woman's body and he was thankful for that. He began walking back toward the plane, following in reverse the notches upon the trees. The smoke from his cigarette slowly disguised the smell of the death that lay behind him. He finished his cigarette just as he came to the crest of the incline.

Martin had exited the plane a few moments before and he was in the process of walking toward the hill, when Frank hit the crest.

Martin waved to him. "Down here, Frank. What'd you find?"

"Be down in a second, buddy. Give this old man some time."

Martin stood at the bottom of the hill and waited while Frank descended. "Well, what's up there?"

"I found a body."

Martin jumped in, "Not Diana?"

"No, don't get excited. It was a man. Pretty much decomposed, but I'm sure it was a man. I take it you didn't find her either?"

As they talked, the sun was moving in a steady pace toward the horizon. Martin shielded his eyes and looked at the descending sun as he spoke, "No, there are a lot of bodies in there and most are in bad shape." He looked back at Frank. "Animals and flies got to 'em. But, I'm sure none of them is my girl."

"You might be right about her making it, Martin. Somebody notched trees in the woods at fairly regular intervals. If she was as knowledgeable about the woods as you say, it might have been her."

Martin started walking back to the Cessna. "Cramer, the NTSB guy, told me there were fifteen confirmed passengers, including a small child and three crew members. I counted thirteen passengers and two crew members."

They had reached the Cessna 152. Frank said, "That means three people survived."

"Yeh, that's how I count it. Minus the guy in the woods, that leaves two. Diana and somebody else."

Martin looked around the area at the desolation and he thought of how it must have looked in the dead of winter. Now it was different, full of life. He wondered why Diana had not come out of the woods yet. Surely, if she had made it through the horrible months of January and February, she could have gotten out by now. He looked at Frank and Frank had a questioning expression on his face.

"I sort of know what you're thinking. Why isn't she out of here, if she's still alive?"

Frank just nodded a 'yes'. He hung on one of the wing struts and rested his body.

"I'm hopeful. I know almost three months have gone by, but she is tough." He paused, and then continued, "I almost lost her once in a canoe accident. She was only eight. Her mother was swept away. My wife's body was never found. I spent months looking." The memories brought tears to Martin's eyes.

"Sorry to hear that buddy."

"Diana was left lonely and afraid. She needs to know that she is loved. I have to find her and bring her home. I can't go through this again and come up empty."

Frank moved away from the plane and stepped to where Martin stood in the grass. "I'll stick with you. We'll find your girl." He patted Martin on the shoulder.

Martin blew air through his lips. "Thanks, Frank." He went to the plane and rummaged in a knapsack behind the pilot's seat and pulled out a roll of a plastic orange fluorescent streamer and a bag of thin wire hooks.

Frank sprang into action. "Where do you want to put it?"

"Might as well put it near the pine arrow."

Martin unrolled a long length of the streamer and he and Frank proceeded to make a large X on the ground. They secured the material with the hooks.

The sun was low and cast long shadows across the field. They finished the task and climbed back into the Cessna 152. Martin ran the plane down the sod field as close as he could to the trees on the other end before he turned the craft back into the wind. He did a check on the carb heat, put the flaps at 30 degrees and then pushed the throttle full ahead. He horsed the plane down the field and pulled the nose up. It gained altitude and skimmed over the treetops and they were up and away.

He yelled above the droning of the engine. "I'm going to fly in the direction the arrow points for a little bit." I'll keep the flaps down so we can fly slower.

Frank looked down into the forest in the dimming light as evening fell. "I see a stream, Martin."

The plane continued flying low and slow. Martin flipped on the navigation lights as darkness descended upon the ground. The sky was still aglow with the fading of sunlight, but below it was pitch black.

Martin continued flying straight south. "If Diana found the creek, she'd follow it."

Frank strained to see. "I can't see the creek anymore, it's too dark."

"Okay, buddy. I give up, for today." He hit a switch and killed the flaps, then pushed the throttle full. The plane gained speed and he banked right and headed back toward the beacon of Hayward field. The engine droned loudly as the Cessna lifted skyward and soared high above the treetops.

Tomorrow would be a day full of activity and discovery.

CHAPTER 31

The fire in the fireplace was almost burned out. Faintly glowing embers revealed the intertwined bodies of Diana and Casey lying on the bed. A blanket was loosely draped over their nude bodies. They were asleep. Outside the sun set and in the fading of the light, a sound reverberated over the trees. It droned louder and louder. Diana sat up and listened.

She recognized the sound as the engine of a small aircraft and it seemed to be low. She got up hurriedly and wrapped the blanket around her body as she opened the door. She was surprised to find that it was almost dark outside. She looked upward in the dwindling light of the sky and saw a wing-tip nav light for a brief second. Then the craft turned and she could not see it anymore.

Diana saw the wolf couple standing near the deer rack and she called to them.

"Did you see it?"

The alpha cocked his head from side to side.

"That was some of my people, trying to find us perhaps. They want to take us back."

The wolf stared at her, then wagged its tail a few strokes and turned away. He and his mate headed for the creek.

Diana shut the door and turned back toward the bed. Casey was sitting up, staring at Diana.

"Who are you talking to?"

"The wolf, who else?" Diana moved toward the fireplace.

Casey looked out the window, "My God, Diana, it's pitch black outside."

"I know." She picked up a poker and prodded the coals. They flared and she put several logs on them. "Our day in bed made us forget a lot of things, like keeping the fire going. If we'd had a blazing one, whoever was in that plane might have spotted us."

Casey stepped out of bed, struggling to pull her pants on.

"A plane flew over?"

"Close by. Close enough for me to see the nav lights. And low too." She poked at the logs.

"Oh, Diana. We'll go back soon, won't we?"

"We could have gone back sooner, but I really didn't want to."

Casey moved to face Diana. "I know. I reached a point where I didn't want to either. I never thought I'd learn to love it here, but I do."

Diana stared into Casey's eyes. "I love you Casey. I'm not sure that I'm ready to go back, but I will because you have to go to your family. And, I have to see my father. We could stay here, you know."

"How could we? What about money and such?"

Diana smiled. "Yeh, I suppose we could use some to fix this up a little. The roof does leak in the corner."

Casey frowned, "Don't make fun. I have a job. At least I guess they would keep it for me."

"I was ready to quit, Casey. I've salted away money for a number of years and with dad's help, made some good investments. We could do okay?"

Casey moved away from the fire and grabbed her shirt off a chair and sat down at the table, her back to Diana.

"There are other things."

"Like what? What other things?" Diana went to the table and sat down.

Casey was afraid to tell her. "I love you."

"I know that. And, I love you."

"That's the problem."

"What is?"

"How can I tell my family that I want to live in the woods with a woman and give up my career and everything?"

"Casey, what are you saying? If you want to keep working, you can. I just want us to be together."

Casey began to cry. "Don't you see? I can't tell my family that I'm in love with a woman. They wouldn't understand. What about your father?"

Diana was dumbfounded and anger began to creep up the back of her neck. "My dad knows about my preference. All he wants is for me to be happy. I've been alone for a long time, until you. I never thought I could love again. I didn't want to, because it hurts when things don't work out. Dammit, Casey, I love you. We can work it out."

"Diana, I can't go back there and live with you. How will I explain it?"

Diana found her pants at the foot of the bed and put them on, along with her flannel shirt. She sat down on the edge of the bed and pulled her boots on. "Remember when I told you that you made me accept the seasons of the heart? The full circle? Everything? I haven't been willing to do that in years because people play so many games. Why do you have to explain love? It just is, isn't it? Do you explain why you love a sister or a brother, or a father or a mother? Or a man or another woman?"

"You make it sound so easy, but it isn't. You've heard the nasty jokes, the way people talk about it."

"You bet I have and when I was a kid, I felt ashamed because those jokes made me feel dirty. Well, dammit, Casey that isn't how it is. I've worked, I've paid taxes, I've done my share of charity work and I've never knowingly hurt anyone in my life. I like me just the way I am."

"Well, I don't want to feel dirty or cheap. I couldn't take it."

"Don't you be the one to tell me that this is wrong. Not now. This isn't something that just happens and then goes away, Casey. You can't tell me that I haven't touched you in ways that you've never been touched before. You know it's right for you."

Casey looked at Diana; her eyes filled with tears. The shadow that had been hidden for all these months was now in the open. "I'm not that strong, Diana. Don't you see, I'm not that strong?"

"You're wrong Casey. Love is strong. It's stronger than any other force in the world. If you love strong enough, then anything is possible. Even us." Diana picked up a blanket and walked out onto the porch.

Casey called after her. "Where are you going?"

"Just down to the creek. I need some time alone. I'll be back." Diana closed the door and stepped off the porch onto the soft pine needles that covered the ground.

Casey pulled the chair over to the fireplace and sat staring at the flames. So much had happened in the past few months. She was at a loss to explain to herself how she had come to love Diana. It had seemed so easy and so natural to her. Much more so, than her marriage had been. Could that be why she had never felt at ease with her husband? A thousand thoughts and fears raced through her mind. She stared into the fire.

Diana wandered down to the creek. The stars shown brightly, but Diana did not see them. For all her life, she had wanted to find the one person who would make her heart sing and her soul rejoice. Yes, she had had other loves, but never one that touched her this deeply. She knew within her heart that she had finally found the person who could be the one for a lifetime, but she knew that she could not fight the fears that dwelled within Casey.

She looked up to the heavens. "Oh, God, how could you be so wrong about love? It's supposed to be the saving grace. Why won't people let it be?"

Off in the distance, the wailing howl of a wolf sounded mournfully through the forest. The smell of burning wood drifted along the treetops. Crickets clamored their high-pitched sounds and frogs grumped along the bank. Somewhere nearby, a whippoorwill called and was answered from a short distance. Diana should have felt as if she was in heaven, but she was lonely and believed that love would pass her by. "Casey. Casey. Casey."

Diana sat by the creek for hours. When she returned to the cabin, Casey was turned on her side toward the wall. Diana slipped into bed and lay on her back, staring at the ceiling.

"Goodnight, Casey."

"Goodnight."

CHAPTER 32

Diana arose early the next day. When the first glimmer of morning light seeped into the window, she could no longer lie awake pretending to sleep. She wondered if Casey had slept, but she did not know, for Casey kept her back to her all night long. She eased out of bed and put some water in the pot to make sassafras tea.

The fire had dwindled during the night to smoldering ashes.

Diana put some large logs on the coals and then went outside to find some wet logs. She stood on the edge of the porch and looked eastward. The sun was creeping over the horizon and shafts of light pierced the forest. It would be a warm, sunny day. She rooted in the woodpile and found some damp cedar logs. She pulled out several and carried them into the cabin.

Casey was standing by the fire. She had already dressed in a flannel shirt and baggy denim pants. She turned as Diana entered.

"Morning, Diana."

Diana approached the fireplace with the logs. She looked directly into Casey's eyes and could see strangeness there. Was it fear? "Good morning. How'd you sleep?"

"Okay."

Damn, it's going to be like that, Diana thought. Strained. Well, she would not press. Diana knew that there was no use in talking about what happened with Casey. For a long time, she had known the same fear that now gripped Casey. It was a fear that could destroy you. It took Diana's father's love to help her overcome the fear of who she was, for all around her, in the little towns of northern Michigan, were constant reminders that she was not normal. She could still hear the words, "queer", "wimp", "sissy", and "faggot" echo in her ears. It had been worse for the boys, but she still had been badgered by questions, "Why aren't you married? Haven't you got a boyfriend?" Cruel questions. Cruel. As if a person could change how she looked at the world and whom she wanted to love. There was so much she wanted to tell Casey, but she did not believe that Casey wanted to hear her now and so, she would play the game of denial.

"I slept okay too." She threw the damp logs on the fire and they belched thick smoke. It drafted up the chimney.

"Why are you doing that?"

Diana put the pot of water containing sassafras roots on the iron arm and swung it over the fire.

"They'll come for us soon. They'll spot the heavy smoke. If not today, then maybe tomorrow." She managed a smile. "We'll be out, back to civilization."

"Yes, back to the real world."

"Yeh. We can drink real coffee and not *Pine Sol* and sassafras tea. And, we can spend our time looking at meaningful television. And pretend that we're happy and contented."

Casey looked at Diana. "I", she hesitated.

Diana looked directly into her eyes.

Casey began again, "I don't want to be hurt or to hurt. I just can't see how we can be together back there. It could ruin me professionally."

"I would give anything to help you learn that you cannot live by the choices that others make for you. Otherwise, you deny your soul. You have to decide what you want and then go after it. If you want it bad enough and if it means everything to you, then it will work out."

Diana poured herself a cup of sassafras tea.

Casey held out her cup. Diana filled it. "I love you, Diana. You know that don't you? I always will. I'll cherish this time forever." She sipped from her cup.

Diana was at a loss. Hurt and anger, both at Casey and at the cruelness of ignorant society, welled within her. How could ignorance cause Casey to be ashamed and regret their love? "If only you could love yourself enough to see that what others try to deny you, is the very thing we all want. Love, acceptance of who we are and what we hope to be. Something permanent, enduring."

Casey said nothing. She averted Diana's gaze.

Diana would not talk about it anymore. She kissed Casey passionately on the mouth and then went to the door. She turned, "I love you, Casey and I always will. No one can take that away from me. Not even you." She closed the door and walked toward the creek.

Casey stood at the window and watched Diana move through the pine trees until she was lost to her sight. She expected Diana to emerge from the pines and go to the rock, but she did not. Casey watched a long time, but she did not see Diana. She went back to the fireplace and sat looking at the flames.

Then, she threw more damp wood onto the fire. The thick black smoke billowed up the chimney.

CHAPTER 33

The Cessna 152 lifted off the runway at Hayward airport just as the sun peaked over the horizon. The field was a maze of activity with planes landing and taking off. Incoming planes carried both FAA and NTSB personnel. A helicopter carrying a coroner and some Army reserves was expected to arrive at mid-morning. The careful inspection of the aircraft and the removal of the bodies was about to begin. Even some of the members of the families who had lost loved ones were beginning to trickle into the small town of Hayward and to make their way to the airport.

Martin looked down on the activity as he lifted skyward.

"Well, Frank. It looks like the day of reckoning is here for Drake. Once they get to the site, those NTSB people will go over that craft with a fine toothcomb. Gene Cramer must be real happy."

"Yeh, I'm glad I'm not in Drake's shoes."

"Drake will get what he deserves." Martin banked the Cessna to the left and headed to the crash site. He planned to follow the arrow until he came to something that might indicate where Diana and the other person could be. Joe and Al had assured him that the area, although desolate, did have old abandoned cabins scattered in some areas of the forest.

Within fifteen minutes, Martin had flown to the site and circled it once to look the area over again, and then he headed south.

Frank peered below. "I can see a creek. It wanders around, but I see it."

They continued to follow the creek. "If Diana found it, she'd follow that thing until dooms day. I hope that didn't happen."

Up ahead perhaps twenty miles from the crash site, a large billow of smoke ascended from the forest. Frank spotted it. "See that Martin? See it?" He looked at his charts. "There's not supposed to be anything out here except animals and trees."

Martin grinned. "You bet I see it. It has to be my girl. It just has to be. Hell, Frank, I bet we were near it last night. She's sending me a signal." He pushed the throttle forward and the airspeed indicator edged up to 140 miles per hour.

"Hey, buddy. Don't blow the engine on this little guy."

Martin eased back a little. "God, I can't help it, Frank. I know she's there waiting for us to get her. I just know it."

The plane flew on toward the smoke and within five minutes they were near the site. Martin banked the plane and did a tight three sixty around the ascending smoke. "Can you see anything?"

"No, pine trees block the cabin, but it's there."

They continued to circle. Martin strained to see any life.

Away from the cabin and the pine trees, a figure ran under the barren canopy of oak and maple branches. The person frantically waved a white piece of cloth. "By God, Frank. Look."

Frank saw the figure and he broke into laughter. He was happy for Martin. "Hey, buddy. We did it. We found them."

"There's only one, though. Do you see another?"

"No, just the one."

Martin frowned, but he believed it had to be Diana. It had to be. He flew away from the site and headed back toward Hayward airport. "Let's get on the ground and try to see if there's any way to get there."

"You bet." Frank had taken a magnetic reading when they turned from the site. He coupled that with the heading that had taken them away from the crash site and now, he had the location of the cabin pretty much pinpointed. "I can get us back there on the ground if the boys have any land maps of this forest."

"Al said they had some hiking maps and some old logging maps of the area. Those will have to do. I'll find that place if it takes all day today and all day tomorrow, but I'll find it. Directed activity, that's what it takes."

Frank smiled. He sort of wished he had served with Martin in Nam. They would have gotten along famously.

Within a short period of time, Martin had returned to Hayward field and had landed. The apron around the shack was loaded with all sorts of aircraft and vehicles, many of which had carried body recovery people and families who had come to claim their loved ones to Hayward field. The parking lot was jammed with cars and with media vehicles. The media trucks already were up and running, their relay dishes extended skyward. Beside the trucks, news people were taping their lead-ins.

Martin and Frank made their way to the shack. An army reserve stood guard at the door. "Sorry sir, only official people are permitted to enter. State your business."

"I've located a survivor and it's my girl. I've been here for months. Frank and I are the ones who found the craft."

"Just a moment sir." The young reservist stepped inside the door and in a moment Gene Cramer came outside.

"Come on in Forrester. Glad to see you. I see your persistence paid off." He slapped Martin on the shoulder and shook his hand. He looked at Frank. "You too. You were the mechanic, huh?"

"Yes, sir." Frank was a little nervous to talk to NTSB people.

Martin spoke. "Gene. Frank was instrumental in helping me locate the plane and my girl. He spent days working on this with me, Joe and Al."

"Don't worry. We know all about Drake's changing the data and service records on that plane." Gene looked at Frank. "You'll be okay. Maybe a few months suspension of your license, but you'll get it back."

Martin smiled. The guy still looked like Woody Allen, but he was a top-notch guy, and fair.

As Gene and Frank moved to the table in the center of the shack, where charts and other papers were laid out in a systematic manner, Joe pulled Martin aside. "I want you meet Brad Nelson. He's from the Chequamegon National Forest Service. He can help you locate trails in the area where you spotted the cabin."

Brad was helping himself to coffee as Joe and Martin moved through the seeming mob of people toward him. After brief introductions, they got down to business and in no time, they were working out a plan to get to the cabin.

Brad said, "We can't get another chopper down here right away or we'd try to get in there with that. But from what Al and Joe say, your girl has everything under control anyway."

"We'll go by land. The maps you gave me will do the job."

"Your girl must be some tough cookie." Brad smiled.

"To tell you the truth, I don't know if it's Diana. I just have a gut feeling."

Joe laughed. "You got my vote and Al's. You made believers out of us."

The familiar smell of a *Macanudo* cigar hit Martin's nostrils and he jerked his head toward the back door. It opened and Carl Drake stepped into the room. Martin said, "Well, son of a bitch."

Carl saw him and hesitated for a moment. "Now look, pal, don't go gettin' punch happy. Your daughter made it from what I hear. You got no beef with me." He quickly circled around the knot of men and moved to the table. He was caught off guard to see Frank seated with Gene going over some records.

Gene looked up. "Just the man I want to see. Sit down."

Carl moved his cigar around in his mouth. He didn't look at Gene, he glared at Frank. "What the hell are you still hangin' around here for?"

Frank glared back at him. "I have the need to see how this all ends."

Gene got edgy. "I said, sit down, Drake. I got a few items to go over with you. And some of these items you won't find real digestible standing up."

Frank looked at Gene. "You'll have to excuse me. I don't like the company here anymore." He got up and moved to where Martin and the other men stood.

Carl sat down at the table, making sure his back was toward Martin and the others. He sat on Gene's right side. He laid his stub of a cigar in the ashtray. "What's the deal? I did nothin' wrong. I'm just a small business guy trying to make an honest buck."

Gene faced him. "That's not quite how it looks. From what Frank has been…"

Carl interrupted, "Shit that drunk doesn't know nothin'. He's a liar if he says he does."

Frank doubled his fists and started to move toward Drake. Martin and Joe grabbed him. Gene motioned for them to hold him.

Carl pulled another cigar from his coat pocket and cut the end off with his pocketknife. He looked defiantly at Gene, as he lit it.

Gene was visibly irritated. "Well, if Frank's a liar, then a whole lot of other people are liars too. Like Hanley and Keane the FAA inspectors. They have been out there for hours now and the reports don't look good for you."

"Hell, hours don't tell ya nothin'. The plane's been there for months. Shit, the weather and animals prowlin' around…You never will be sure what happened." He blew a large cloud of smoke.

Gene coughed. "It might take us months to reconstruct it, but I know this right now. You are in for one hell of a law suit and if I have anything to say about it, you won't ever own an airline again."

"Say, don't go settin' yourself up as no judge and jury, pal. You're nothin' but a two-bit government worker. I know senators who'll take care of you so fast that you'll be glad to keep a job cleaning toilets at the local post office." Drake blew smoke in Cramer's face.

Gene coughed again. "I've got a job to do. You can threaten all you want, but in the end, I'll decide your fate. You're history in this business. And, don't blow that damn smoke in my face again."

"History my ass. Money talks. Not your cheap little government job, pal. I'll be in this business long after you're gone." He blew an enormous wad of smoke in Gene's face.

Cramer exploded. "My boss wouldn't like what I'm about to do but if it costs me my job, I'm going to have the last word." He stood tall and delivered a smashing blow to Drake's nose just as Drake was about to take another puff on his *Macanudo*. Drake was knocked off his chair and landed flat on his back on the floor; the cigar clutched firming in his hand.

Martin and the others in the room were stunned. Martin looked at Cramer and saw Woody Allen turn into John Wayne. He burst out laughing.

"Damn. This guy just doesn't have any kind of smoking etiquette." Martin looked at Gene. "You delivered your last word quite well. My compliments." He saluted Gene.

Cramer smiled a Woody Allen smile.

Martin motioned to Frank. "Come on, Frank. There's plenty of time for you to get a final word with Drake. He just doesn't seem to get the message. He's bound to screw up again."

Martin and Frank walked outside into the warm sun of late morning. They had a plan and thanks to Al and Joe, the vehicles to do the job. And, thanks to the Forest Service, they had the maps to locate the cabin. The saga was coming full circle.

Martin smiled as a warm breeze ruffled his dark hair. He ran his right hand through it and smoothed it down again.

CHAPTER 34

Diana had crossed the creek in the early morning and had walked aimlessly in the woods, not really seeing anything. She tried to piece together what had happened and what had gone wrong. Falling in love with Casey had not been easy, it had just happened, in spite of all of her fears and a remembrance of old hurts.

She crossed another creek and came to a field. The new shoots of prairie grass had burst through the warming soil and were several inches high. The old grass from last year lay matted and soft in the sun. Diana looked overhead and saw a hawk circling lazily in the same warm easy breeze that whispered through the nearby pines. Cottony clouds moved slowly through the azure sky. The mid-morning sun felt warm.

She sat down in the field just as the familiar keening sound of a killdeer sounded. She saw the plover running in the short blades of grass, searching for an open dirt place to lay its eggs. She turned from that to study some ladybugs for a few moments, as they crawled in little spurts of energy up the new shoots of prairie grass. She felt drowsy in the warming sun. Soon its blanket of warmth enveloped her and Diana lie down in the soft grass and fell asleep.

Casey busied herself with trying to clean the cabin. She had no idea why she was doing this. What difference would it make? In just a matter of a short time, someone would come for them and they would be out of this place. She set the scraggly broom aside and walked out onto the cabin porch. The rising sun pierced the pine canopy and sent sharp shafts of mid-morning sunlight to dance on the pine needles that covered the ground around the cabin.

She stood on the porch and looked toward the creek. She could not see Diana and she wondered where she had gone. She stepped off the porch, walked past the deer rack and pushed her way through the small pines and headed toward the big rock. She easily made the jump from land to the flat piece of granite that jutted out into the small stream. She remembered the first time she had watched Diana sit on this same rock and bath. Had it been so long ago?

Casey sat down crossed legged and rested her head on her knees. She looked into the water and saw some trout drifting lazily in the little eddies that swirled around the boulder. To her, they looked so graceful, so pretty and so free. The sunlight beat upon her head and warmed her whole being. The rock was hard, but she did not care, for she was tired. She stretched out on the flat, water-smoothed surface of the rock and in a matter of moments, fell asleep.

Martin and Frank had taken the rest of the morning to prepare for the trip into the forested area where they had seen the smoke from the cabin. Joe and Al had secured some *Yamaha* 4x4 ATV's from a local dealer and by noon, the vehicles were packed with a few supplies and loaded onto trailers for transport to the drop-off site. Martin would pull one of the trailers with his rented *Bronco* and Joe had volunteered to haul the second one with his truck.

Martin was silent as they headed to the drop-off point. He followed Joe down winding paved roads, turning left and right onto other paved roads and finally turning onto dirt logging roads that snaked through what seemed to Martin to be an endless forest. Finally, he spoke to Frank, "It's no wonder Diana didn't get out. I'm not sure I can even drive back to town."

Frank smiled. Martin had seemed tense for most of the drive and it had bothered him, but now as Joe braked to a stop, in preparation to unload the ATV's, Martin seemed to return to life.

"It'll be all right. We'll find them."

The logging road that they had stopped on had just come to an abrupt end in the woods. Joe grinned as he jumped out of his truck. "This is it, boys. Some forest, huh?"

"One hell of a forest." Martin began to untie the rope and cords that held the ATV's on the trailers. Once that was done, he went to the *Bronco* and got maps and charts and spread them out on the hood.

"I need to get my bearings, fellows. Can you handle the rest?"

"You bet," Frank answered.

Martin took some compass readings and made some notations on the maps. By the time he was finished, Joe and Frank had the vehicles unloaded and ready.

Joe spoke. "You're all set, buddy. Good luck. I'll leave my trailer here." He extended his hand to Martin.

"I can't tell you how much this means to me."

"I know." Joe looked Martin square in the eyes. "Hope to see you and your girl before night fall. Now hit it. You're losing light."

Martin straddled the *Yamaha, Timberwolf,* and with Frank roaring to go on his own, Martin led the way off into the woods. Frank followed a short distance behind. Joe watched them leave and then he hopped into his truck and headed back to Hayward.

The noise from the vehicles sent squirrels and chipmunks running for safety. The loggers had left scattered brush throughout the forest and sometimes Martin had to retrace some paths in order to get around the debris. He constantly looked at his watch. The time seemed to move at two speeds, slow in finding the cabin and fast in losing the light of day. He stopped periodically to check the maps and to look at his compass. He made notations on the charts and then moved ahead again. Frank followed.

Several hours after they had left the logging road, Martin stopped and shut off his engine. He motioned for Frank to do the same.

Frank shut down and walked up to Martin. "What's up?"

"I want to listen. Maybe we can hear something." Martin scanned the area, but saw nothing out of the ordinary. He listened intently, the engine noise still echoed in his ears. After several minutes of standing still, he looked at Frank. "You hear that?"

"Hear what? I don't hear anything but critters running around."

"Listen. It sounds like a stream." Martin began walking and then running toward the right. Forty yards from where Frank stood by the ATV's, Martin found a stream. He let out a whoop.

Frank yelled to him. "What is it?"

"It's a creek. This has to be it. We're headed in the right direction." He walked back to Frank.

Frank smiled. He checked his watch. "Well, it's two-thirty. If we find the cabin soon, we can get back before dark."

Martin grinned. "As Joe says, 'let's hit it.'"

They moved closer to the stream, which lay at the foot of a small incline and followed it northward, paralleling its twists and turns for another half hour.

Then, in front of Martin, the ground dipped downward and almost at the same time, he saw the cabin and the creek. On a rock in the creek a lone figure of a woman lay curled. His heart pounded.

Casey awoke from a dream and was startled to hear the noise from the vehicles and then to see the two men approach. She stood up.

Martin could see the thin body of a woman, frail looking, and yet somehow robust. His heart sank. It was not Diana. He smiled at her as he stopped the ATV.

Casey looked at Martin and knew that he had to be Diana's father. The same curly dark hair and the same smile. She walked up the gentle slope from the creek to where he had stopped near the small pines. Tears welled in her violet eyes.

"You must be Diana's father?"

Martin wanted to hug this woman, but he only extended his hand. "Yes. Where is she? Is she okay?"

The months of struggle finally hit her and the pent up emotions suddenly burst. She began to cry and sob.

Martin put his arms around her and pulled her close, not knowing what she meant by all this emotion. "You'll be okay. But, please, where is Diana?"

"I don't know. She's fine. She'll be here soon. She went off into the woods."

Martin held her for a few more moments as her sobbing continued. He motioned to Frank and Frank took a pack of food off the rack on the ATV. "Come on, little bit. Let's go see where you've been living."

Casey wiped her nose across her flannel shirtsleeve and started to laugh. "I'm Casey. I'm glad you found us."

"And, I'm Martin. This other big guy is Frank." The three of them walked through the pines and up to the cabin. Frank carried a small package of canned soups and a jar of instant coffee.

As Casey stepped on the cabin porch she said, "It isn't much, but it saved us."

Martin looked inside. "Well, I see you have a fire and a kettle hanging over it. How about some coffee? It's instant, but it's good."

"I don't care if it's instant. We haven't had anything but *Pine Sol* and rosehip tea to drink for ages. I'd love some coffee."

The three of them went inside the cabin.

Martin could see that the bed was laced with a garland of pine boughs and dried flowers from last fall. He looked around the cabin and saw that it was warm and cozy and that the table had a small bouquet of pussy willows. He looked at this woman, Casey, and he knew all there was to know about his daughter and this relationship. He smiled.

She smiled at him, as she poured water into the kettle and swung it over the fire.

He sat down at the wooden table and smiled back at her.

For a short length of time, all three sat drinking coffee, while Casey filled in the details of the crash and their struggle for survival. She told of the axe cut and of how Diana had sewed her leg. Martin marveled at the courage of this woman and of the way his daughter had handled all that had been thrown at her.

"It must have been hard, but now it's over."

Casey looked at him. "Yes, now it's over."

From outside came the yell, "Dad! Dad?"

Martin jumped to his feet and ran outside. Diana was just coming through the small pines from the creek. He ran to her. "Oh, thank God. I knew you'd make it. I just knew it. Oh, baby, I love you!"

Diana threw herself in her father's arms and wept.

Casey sat on the porch steps and watched the scene. How much they seemed alike. So strong, so sure of life. She watched as they talked to one another. Martin looked up toward Casey a few times and then went back to listening to whatever it was that Diana was saying.

Frank leaned against a porch post and smoked a cigarette.

Father and daughter stopped talking and walked back to where Casey and Frank waited.

Diana caught sight of Frank. "Oh, my God, Frank. It's good to see you."

Frank stepped down and embraced Diana. "It's good to see you too. Damn, I'm glad you made it." He smiled at her, as tears formed in the corners of his eyes.

Martin said. "Well, it appears that we need to head back. We'll run out of day light, if we don't hurry." He looked at Casey. "I believe your parents are waiting back at the terminal. Nobody knew who the other person was that made it. They just knew it was a woman with Diana. Your last name is Morgan, isn't it?"

Casey looked in disbelief. "Yes. Yes." She hesitated, and then continued. "They came here?"

"Sure did. They're staying at the same motel I'm at."

Casey looked at Diana.

Martin saw the exchange and motioned Frank to walk with him down to where they had left the ATV's.

When the men were out of hearing distance, Diana spoke. "I'm not going back for a few days. Dad brought some things to eat. I'll be okay. I just need time to adjust and time to think." She wanted to grab Casey and kiss her, but she didn't.

Casey stared at her. "You're not going back? I…I don't know what to say. I thought I'd jump for joy to be going home, but…"

"Oh, it's just pre-partum blues." Diana worked at smiling. "We've been here so long. You know?"

Casey stared at her. "I'll miss you."

"Yeh. I'll miss you." Diana stared at Casey. "I told my dad to come back for me in a couple of days." She moved to the cabin porch.

Casey went to Diana and put her arms around her. "Please understand. I have to go. I don't know how to deal with us." She hugged Diana.

Diana felt stiff and she did not want to, not with this woman. She relented and hugged Casey, and then she kissed her cheek. She could smell her hair as she whispered. "Go, then. I'll be okay. But, know that I will always love you. That will never change. Not now. Not ever." She broke the embrace and walked with Casey down to where her father and Frank stood waiting.

Martin spoke to Casey. "Ready to go?"

"Yes." She looked at Diana.

"Take care of her, Dad. She's been through some rough times."

"I'll take care of her, Diana. Just like she was my own." He winked a loving wink. "I'll be back in two days."

Diana watched as Casey sat behind her father. The engines started and then Frank and Martin turned the machines around to follow the tracks that they had left in the soft earth of the warm April day. Soon they would be back to the drop-off place. Long after they had disappeared from view, Diana could still hear the faint rumble of the engines.

She walked back to the cabin and sat down on the porch. It was so quiet, now. Only bird songs and the chatter of squirrels sounded in the woods. No voice called her name. She looked down toward the creek and saw the wolf and its mate coming through the pines toward the cabin. Behind them, followed two little pups.

Diana said out loud, "I'll be damned. I wish Casey could see this. They did make this their home."

She watched as the family came toward the cabin. The male alpha saw her and stopped. He seemed to smile a proud smile and then he led his family off into the seclusion of the large pines and blossoming red maples of the forest.

Diana sat on the porch for a long time and looked at the world that moved around her. She saw mourning doves and blue jays and crows and chipmunks. They moved freely through their world. She sat there all afternoon. Then, as the sun set, she went inside the cabin and closed the door.

A wailing sound echoed through the forest and made the animals stop their movement. The sound was more mournful and primal than the howling of the wolf, for it was the embodiment of loneliness and despair.

The continued wailing shook the alpha wolf and he howled as if to soothe the soul who called into the night. But there was no solace for the human who lived inside the cabin, so the wolf stopped his howling and went back into the forest to his family.

In time, the night was silent.

CHAPTER 35

❀

The following morning, Diana spent hours scouring the woods, looking at the marsh areas, finding trillium and delighting in the return of the redwing blackbirds, the robins and the bluebirds. She wandered through the woods, touching the fir trees, smelling the pinecones and bathing in the cold water of the small stream.

While she sat drying herself on the rock, the wolves came and the small pups trailed behind the alpha pair. Diana wanted to hold a pup, but she knew that although the adults tolerated her presence, the female would attack her if she even moved toward the babies. The family had come down by the stream, near the large pine and fir trees that lined the bank opposite the rock to drink. They eyed her, but never showed any fear or aggression. She talked to them and they turned their heads as though listening to her words, but it was a game that only Diana understood. They had their fill of water and then wandered back into the pines.

She thought of Casey often and when she did, the loneliness and the emptiness of the place overwhelmed her. She tried to block out the feelings, but couldn't and so she walked and thought and studied the place. She knew that all too soon her father would come and take her away from this world that had represented love and freedom for the past few months. She believed that she would probably never come this way again. To her, nothing seemed to be permanent anymore, not even a love that invaded your heart and eclipsed it. She wondered what Casey would do and where she would go. Then Diana remembered that they had never even exchanged any kind of address. Casey would be lost forever. And forever was a long, long time.

On the second day, Diana awoke early and sat on the bed studying the cabin. The room was small and yet it had seemed big and full of life when they had shared it together. The bouquet of pussy willows still adorned the table and the garland of dried flowers and pine boughs circled the bed, but they only made Diana sad. She climbed out of bed and pulled on her clothes. The kettle hung over the embers in the fireplace and a slow stream of vapor arose from it. Diana took time to make herself a cup of coffee before she walked outside into the early morning light.

It was a warm sunny morning and the constant chirping of the sparrows and the familiar song of a cardinal punctuated the air. The smell of pine was all around her. She looked over near the deer rack and spotted the double bit ax which was still stuck in the log where she had split wood. She smiled in remembering when Casey had found it. "Damn," she muttered aloud. "Damn. Why does life have to be so complicated?"

She set the empty coffee cup on the porch and walked down toward the creek. The wolves were nowhere to be seen. She crossed the stream and headed toward the meadow that she had found two days ago. As she came out of the woods which rimmed the meadow, she saw a herd of deer grazing on the far side. She stopped in the shadows of the pines and watched them. A large buck sniffed the air and turned his head in her direction, his ears alert. The others stopped grazing and turned toward her and sniffed the air. She knew she'd been found out, so she stepped out into the sunlight. They stared at her a moment and then bounded and leaped into the woods. Their white tails bobbed as they disappeared among the trees.

It was a beautiful day and Diana had nowhere to go, not yet, anyway. She decided to just lie in the grass and watch clouds or hawks pass overhead. And, so she did. As always, Casey was in the back of her mind.

Diana did not know how long she stayed in the meadow, but she knew by the lengthening shadows that it had been for many hours. It was time to go back to the cabin to join her father and return to civilization.

She wandered back through the forest and came to the log that crossed the creek. When she got close to the rock, she could see an ATV parked near the cabin. She yelled out. "Dad, Dad!"

There was no answer.

Diana noticed that there was a large amount of smoke coming from the chimney and wondered why her father would put more wood on the fire. She mounted the porch and opened the door.

Casey turned from the fireplace and smiled. "Welcome home. I've fixed supper. Later on, you can have dessert or if you wish some 'directed activity.'" She ceremoniously flung half of the blanket that covered her body aside and revealed that she wore nothing.

From down by the creek came the howling of the wolf family. The noise reverberated through the forest.

Diana was astonished at the sight of Casey and what her presence meant. She quietly shut the door of the cabin. She blew air through her teeth and said, "Sweet Jesus. I am undone."

Casey looked at her and winked, "Permanently."

The End

978-0-595-35475-7
0-595-35475-0

Printed in the United States
39301LVS00011B/27

9 780595 354757